THE
ATROCITY
BELLS

Join our mailing list at

palmcirclepressbooks.com

For news about upcoming releases, exclusive previews, and special subscriber-only content!

This is a work of fiction. Names, characters, places, and incidents either are products
of the writer's imagination or are used fictitiously. Any resemblance to actual events
or locales or persons, living or dead, is entirely coincidental.

Printed in the United States of America
ISBN: 979-8-9888754-3-7

Map of Jyn Designed by Peter de Jong

Front Cover Design by Terrence Mercer

Interior Layout by Rachel Newhouse for elfinpen designs

Published by Palm Circle Press
www.palmcirclepressbooks.com

THE LOST BOOKS OF JYN

BOOK ONE

THE
ATROCITY
BELLS

LEE ANDERSON

For Edward

DRAMATIS PERSONAE

~ The Kingdom of Tartaria ~

King Khilji, the King of Tartaria, the Northern Kingdom.
Queen Abika, the Queen of Tartaria.
Princess Sarna, daughter of King Khilji and Queen Abika.
Prince Shayan, son of King Khilji and Queen Abika.
Lalya, Princess Sarna's best friend and schoolmate.
Ohmaar, advisor to King Khilji.
Luca, an ex-soldier turned outlaw who kidnaps Princess Sarna.

~ The Kingdom of the Cathyrnee ~

Chief Arlyn, leader of the Cathyrnee, a nomadic tribe.
Chieftess Yarlaa, wife to Chief Arlyn.
Gish, commander of the Cathyrnee warriors.

~ The Kingdom of Burnya ~

King Montrose, King of Burnya, the Western Kingdom.
Queen Saraal, Queen of Burnya.
Ozyan, handmaiden to Queen Saraal / King Montrose's mistress.
Artemis, Burnya's Gold Master.

~ Shamans, Warlocks, and Spirits ~

Baal, a deity of the ancient underworld, known for demanding ritual sacrifice in exchange for good fortune.

Corsika, a female Ghe-sui shaman, loyal to Chieftess Yarlaa.

Fhamtem, tribal leader of the Chotgor, a race of volcanic beings created by The Great Awakening.

The Magshaa, Master of the Ghe-sui, a shaman cult.

Momaset, leader of the Ghe-sui, spiritual authority second only to The Magshaa.

Seelskan, a high-ranking warlock of the Dark Shulam, a branch of the Ghe-sui devoted to its darker side.

Ulaan, a female Ghe-sui shaman, spiritual counselor to Queen Saraal.

~ Terminology ~

Babsulisk, a popular narcotic fruit juice, extracted from the babsulisk plant.

Drakksuk, flying reptilian creatures with bat wings who breathe lightning.

The Great Awakening, a sudden, mysterious growth spurt in philosophical knowledge, engineering advancement, and psychic abilities.

Ha'wiih, a respectful way of addressing any Cathyrnee leader.

Joppa, a curse word, often used to express anger, frustration, or amazement.

Sünsü, a mysterious energy appearing in Jyn as part of the Great Awakening.

Yelkin, man-eating giants from the Oroo Mountains.

Note about the language:

As could be imagined of an ancient world, the people of Jyn did not speak English, but a language called Xhenkhel. It was the official language of Jyn and the most widely spoken, best-known member of the Xhengolic language family. Speakers across every dialect numbered close to fifteen million, including the vast majority of Jyn civilians and many of the tribal residents of the outer plains and mountains.

While it was possible to recover more than eighty percent of the text's implied connotation, translating Xhenkhel into English involved centuries of specific idioms. Special skill was used to maintain allegiance with the intent and meaning of the original books. However, modern English vernacular was used where appropriate.

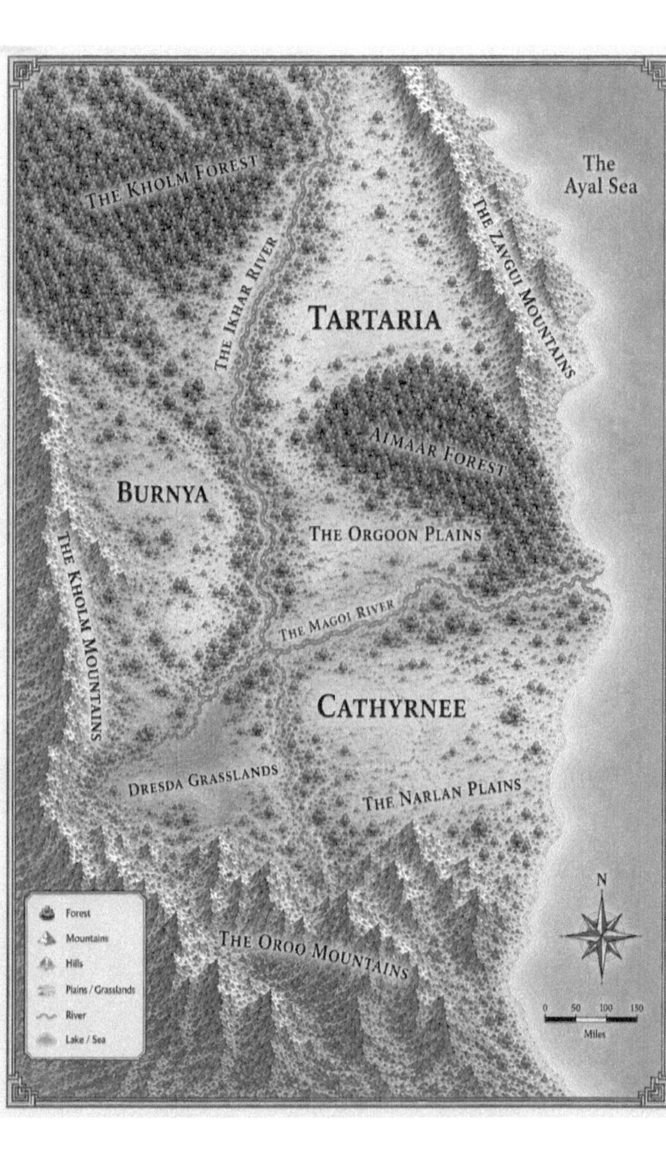

THE KHOLM FOREST
The Ayal Sea
THE IKHAR RIVER
TARTARIA
THE ZAVGUI MOUNTAINS
AIMAAR FOREST
BURNYA
THE ORGOON PLAINS
THE KHOLM MOUNTAINS
THE MAGOI RIVER
CATHYRNEE
DRESDA GRASSLANDS
THE NARLAN PLAINS
THE OROO MOUNTAINS
N
Forest
Mountains
Hills
Plains / Grasslands
River
Lake / Sea
0   50   100   150
Miles

SARNA

Sarna spotted someone watching her. Her school group approached a low sandstone bridge, and she saw the top half of a man's face there, peeking from over the parapet. Sarna stopped walking.

By her side, her dearest friend Lalya stopped too. "My love, what's the matter?" she asked her.

"I saw someone."

"Where?"

"Up there. He ducked back down."

They were part of an all-female art class. Each student held a sketchpad made from linen rags. It wasn't until a few days ago that the class would even brave these field trips, though they never veered far from the kingdom walls. It was still a somewhat risky outing because of the princess, but Sarna had assured the headmaster it was fine, so long as they brought guards. It would be worth it to get some grass between their toes and catch some fresh air.

Naturally, Sarna had been offered private tutoring but preferred being treated like anyone else, weary of the castle's isolation. She even wore the same dark-blue tunic as the other girls, the same gold threadwork.

Six knights protected the class, riding horseback with two in the lead, two astride, and two watching their flank. The students walked single file down a narrow, forested path led by Master Reglan, an elderly teacher with wild, white hair.

Sarna heard a quick zing, then an airless gasp. The front guard clutched at an arrow, which had pierced his throat. He made a gurgling noise and toppled from his horse. The class screamed. A second arrow skewered the eye of the guard behind him, yet another arrow bouncing off his helmet. A fourth arrow punctured his neck, and he too spilled to the ground. He fell with a clanging thud.

Screaming louder, the class dropped their sketchpads and ran back up the trail. Master Reglan remained, immobilized from shock. Sarna and Lalya also stayed, inadvertently blocked by the two rear guards who fought to control their horses while also unsheathing their swords. Before the guards could establish a defensive stance, men with swords and axes erupted from the foliage. Outnumbered, the guards were swiftly stabbed and hacked, then discarded to die in the grass.

Lalya clenched Sarna's arm so hard it hurt. Her friend sobbed hysterically as the bandits surrounded them. The bandits were a dozen strong, at least. Every man became focused on Sarna. They were obviously informed about who she was.

Realizing no one cared about him, Master Reglan fled back up the trail after the other girls. In his panic, he fell several times but eventually disappeared around a corner.

The bandits closed around Sarna and Lalya, forcing them to shrink their space until they embraced one another. The bandits grinned, made cocky by the easy success of their attack, pleased by the terror they were causing.

Sarna could tell by their armor that they were former soldiers of the Great War. Since the conflict had ended, many of these unemployed soldiers had turned to banditry to survive.

"Your Highness," a bandit called to her.

The voice came from atop the leafy arch of the bridge. Sarna realized this was who she'd seen peeking at her. This bandit wore a gray, cotton-padded tunic with a brown sash around the waist, a quiver of arrows riding his back. She noticed the bow in his hand and understood he'd been the archer who killed the first two guards.

"Don't hurt us," Sarna said to him. "Please."

"Don't give us a reason to, and that won't be a problem, Your Highness."

"Let my friend go? You don't need her. I'm the one you want, right?"

Lalya whimpered from the attention. She hid her face in Sarna's shoulder, horrified from even being looked at.

"No, we'll be keeping her, too," the bandit on the bridge said.

One of the men pinched Lalya's thigh. She yelped and scrambled to Sarna's other side, nearly slipping on an abandoned sketchpad. The area was littered with them.

Sarna turned on her friend's assaulter. "Don't touch her! Don't you dare!" She used her arms to shield her friend.

The bandits laughed. Sarna could see that having these spoiled royal bitches at their mercy was hilarious for them.

"Control yourselves!" the archer commanded his men, apparently their leader. He motioned his hands down, a signal for calm. "We talked about this. We have to do this the right way."

"What's the right way?" Sarna asked him. "We'll hide with you somewhere while you wait for a response to your ransom note?"

The bandits' leader nodded. He grinned, bemused. "Something like that. Yeah, let's do that. Good idea, Your Highness."

"My father will hunt you down if it takes him the rest of his life."

More laughter. Sarna felt a hand on her rear, and

she spun away. The molesting bandit grinned at her with yellow-brown teeth, and it was those teeth which somehow made her understand just how perilous their situation was. These men could do whatever they wanted, and there truly wasn't much she could do about it.

Another bandit reached for her, and she backed even further away. The men cheered.

"'Easy,' I said!" the bandit leader called. "The money is more important. The king isn't likely to hand over a ransom without his precious daughter unharmed. Isn't that right, Princess?"

Sarna swallowed hard and nodded empathetically. "Yes, that is very true. Either of us."

"Is this really the princess?" asked another, blocked to her by the others. "How could she be caught so easy? Maybe this is a decoy princess."

Their leader seemed entertained by this notion. "Are you the real Princess Sarna? Or the fake one?" he asked her.

In her nervousness, she considered agreeing to the "fake-ness" idea but decided against it. Her being the real princess was likely the only reason they were still alive and unharmed.

She took Lalya's hand and led her as she nudged their way free from the circle of men. She suffered a pinch here and there but kept walking until she reached the bottom of the small bridge. She looked up at the bandit leader. "Yes, I am the real Princess Sarna. And who are you?"

"My name's Luca. I've been waiting a long, long, long time to meet you, Your Highness."

Sarna turned at the sound of Lalya crying out. A bandit had grabbed her from behind while working a hand inside her tunic. A second bandit grabbed her hair.

"Let go of her!" Sarna yelled. She slapped at them.

"Listen to the princess!" Luca called. "Cut it out!"

The bandits became more excited. The situation was a breath away from fully escalating. "Hey! Hey!" Luca kept shouting. Finally, the men stopped to look up at him. They frowned.

Luca scooted onto his haunches and jumped down from the bridge. He landed on his feet, a graceful brute. He came closer to everyone.

"What did I already say to all of you?" he asked his men.

The men traded glances, seemingly unaware of what anyone had ever said to them about anything. "I told you to listen to what I tell you," Luca continued, "and this will go perfectly smooth. But you have to keep calm. Be smart. Don't get so crazy." He sauntered closer to Sarna, and she could smell him. He smelled earthy with a trace of musk and sweat. "See? Everything's going to be fine, Your Highness. Your father gives us what we want, and no harm will come to you. I guarantee it."

"I don't believe you."

"Does it matter?"

Sarna looked around at the smelly, cockeyed, slobbering pigs around her. She looked at Lalya, then back at Luca. No, it didn't matter.

"I have to confess something." He bent down and picked up the decapitated head of a guard. He looked it over as if considering it for purchase. "You're not what I was expecting," he told her.

She tried her best to ignore the object in his hands. "Look, I understand why you're doing this." She surprised herself with how undisturbed she managed to sound. "I don't necessarily agree with every economic policy my father has ever come up with."

"That so? Those are big words for a young girl. What are you, sixteen?"

"Seventeen."

A shout came from a bandit stationed further up the trail. Someone was coming. Her rescue, perhaps. The bandits had lingered too long.

Before Sarna could react, Luca dropped the severed head and lifted her over his shoulder. He ran with her. She squirmed, but he was too strong. When she tried raising her head to check on Lalya, she didn't see her anywhere. As the bandit ran with her into the woods, sheltered by his men, she bounced on his shoulder like a sack of straw. Branches whipped at her face, so she lowered her head. She went limp and closed her eyes, surrendering to her fate for now. She didn't know what else to do.

SHAYAN

Sarna's brother, the young Prince Shayan, entered the king's chambers, an immense room with a beamed ceiling and stone inner walkway. There were large windows on all four walls, which offered sweeping views of the kingdom and countryside. Handcrafted furniture complemented an enormous, paneled dais bed, the headwall adorned with armor worn by the king in past battles.

Shayan was astonished to find his father undressed and still in bed. There was once a time when King Khilji would have arisen before dawn, accomplishing more before daylight than most men would in their entire week. Those days had expired, apparently.

Ohmaar, King Khilji's advisor for the last six years—before his own father retired from having been the king's hand for nearly his entire life—sat in the corner at a small reading table. He looked morose. Something was off. Both men appeared listless.

"Father," Shayan said, "is everything all right?"

King Khilji edged to the side of his bed. He placed his feet on the floor. "Shayan," he said, "everything is perfect. Why do you bother me?"

"I told you I was coming to speak with you this morning. About our situation with the Cathyrnee and the yelkin. Do you not remember?"

The king spoke over him while pushing himself to his feet: "Spare me! To hell with the Cathyrnee. *Joppa!* Why do you keep bothering me about them?"

Shayan raised his brows, threw a look at Ohmaar. The advisor sat with his fingers laced and shrugged helplessly. "Father, I keep bothering you because they're about to be wiped out," the prince said. "Finished. Gone. Not one more of them."

"Didn't we just defeat them in a Great War? Are they our friends now? Our kingdom has its own problems."

Shayan closed his eyes and inhaled slowly. This had been happening far too often lately. He would hold entire conversations with his father, only to have to repeat everything he'd said the next day. Or even the same evening. Was the relentless pressure placed on the king catching up to him? King Khilji wasn't so old, though lately, he moved with the slow deliberateness of someone twice his age. His stubble was well on its way to becoming a beard, and he'd never grown a beard. "Father, this is not what you said yesterday."

"Yesterday? I didn't see you yesterday."

"You did, and you said I should speak with Chief Arlyn. See what aid we could offer them. It's the humane thing to do. They're so weakened from the war, they're getting attacked and slaughtered by the yelkin. Almost daily."

"What is a yelkin?"

Shayan had to focus on maintaining his composure. What are *yelkin?* Had his father actually asked that? The prince cleared his throat. "They're giant creatures from the mountains. They've all but completely destroyed the Cathyrnee. If we don't help them—"

"Good! Praise the yelkin! I would adore it if they killed off the Cathyrnee! That's what I wanted to do in the first place."

"I understand they're not your favorite people, Father. Mine either. But this isn't right. Letting them just get massacred like that. They're human beings."

King Khilji walked past his son. He gave his shoulder a quick, hard slap. "You're too burdened with your emotions. The Cathyrnee are still our enemies, and they deserve no sympathy. I regret not having them all killed, even the women and children. I don't know how I was talked out of it."

"Because we're not barbarians, Father. If you ask me, the real enemy anymore is Burnya. They made out handsomely from sitting aside and watching us kill each other."

Another glance at Ohmaar. This time, Ohmaar took his eyes to the floor and frowned, embarrassed, having no idea what to do or say. The useless twit. Some advisor.

Shayan pondered if continuing this discussion was even worth it. Or would the king once more dismiss everything being said to him, only a few hours from now? What was going on with him?

"We have to help these people," the prince said. "Or make the attempt. I assume I will have to go over this same speech later today?"

The king had nearly reached a window to look out of but about-faced on his son. "Don't talk to your father like that! The throne isn't yours yet."

The shock of hearing his father say this to him was enough to make the prince take two large steps backward. Prince Shayan started to point out the absurdity of what his father was accusing him of, then felt the futility of this. "I'm going to meet with Chief Arlyn," he said. "See how bad it is. That's all."

"Meet with him? Why? So you can both plot against me?"

"*Plot?* Father—"

"I already know you want me dead. You just can't wait to be king, can you?"

"How could you even *speak* such a thing?"

Another hard glare at Ohmaar brought the advisor to his feet. "My Lord, I think what Prince Shayan—"

The king cut him off, still addressing his son: "Answer me! You want me dead, don't you?"

Shayan held his hands up. "Father, everything I do—and I do mean every single living thing I do, from the moment I awake to the moment I sleep—is for the benefit of our family and this kingdom. No other concern occupies my mind. *Ever.*"

King Khilji responded with such vitriol that the spittle flew from his lips. "I already know everything! I've known it for years now!"

The king collapsed onto his bed and kicked his feet in the air until this seemed to wear him out. Sniffling, running a finger beneath his nose, he lay there while gazing at the ceiling. He cleared his throat and said, "Ohmaar, bring me some tea."

Ohmaar looked back and forth between father and son. "Now, My Lord?"

"No, tomorrow! Yes, now! Bumbling knave! Move!"

King Khilji reached beneath the bed and lifted the chamber pot from there. He threw it, empty thankfully, and it missed Ohmaar by several feet, though not before violently indenting a set of velvet curtains. The pot clattered and rolled to a rest at Prince Shayan's feet.

2

CHIEF ARLYN

The Chief of the Cathyrnee awoke with a start, having fallen asleep by accident. The cool night air touched his bare chest. He lay with his wife, Chieftess Yarlaa, in a round hut with a collapsible wooden frame, covered in felt made from sheep's wool. He reached for Yarlaa beside him, felt her hip beneath layers of fox fur.

A tremor moved through the ground, and Arlyn knew instantly what this meant.

"Yarlaa, wake up." He shook her shoulder. "Yarlaa!"

She raised her head, still deep asleep, her hair a nest of tangles. She mumbled.

"They're here again!" Arlyn got onto his knees to grab her. Carry her if he had to.

A pair of attendant warriors rushed into the hut, their broadswords drawn. "We have to get you to safety!" one of them bellowed.

Their roof lifted off and exposed a dark and stormy sky. A yelkin held the shredded remnants of the roof in its long claws. Tall as any tree, the giant's demented, drooling face was like something drawn by a child, its thick, red hide zigzagged with lacerations from previous battles. The yelkin were made up of spindly, red bodies with long, thin arms, claws nearly reaching the ground. Their legs bent backward like the hind legs of an animal. Their mouths peeled back into perpetual grins, showing rows of yellow fangs inside black gums. An immense pair of horns bracketed their heads.

A section of the roof fell away and narrowly missed crushing all of them. Yarlaa cowered with her arms folded over her head. Arlyn lay on top of her. The nearest warrior rushed and stood above them both. Arlyn slid lower and searched for his sword, cursing his carelessness for not keeping it closer. The long, red arm of the giant creature reached in. The warrior dove to swipe at the arm, but his sword merely bounced off. The blade broke and struck him across the brow. He fell back and clutched his hemorrhaging face. The other warrior was already there to take his place, but a second yelkin approached the open structure. It lifted the man with one hand and sank its teeth into his torso, tearing him in half, entrails gushing loose.

Chief Arlyn and Yarlaa were soon surrounded by the shrieks of people meeting similar deaths. Caught in a feeding frenzy, the yelkin roared from every direction. A horned giant reached inside for Yarlaa. Chief Arlyn cried out for his wife and raised his sword above his head. He brought his blade down across the giant's forearm.

SHAYAN

The prince sat with his father's counselors in the Great Hall, intended as both the main meeting and dining areas, and used by almost anyone who lived in the castle for almost any reason. The Great Hall was a large one-room structure with a loft ceiling located in the Inner Ward. At the end sat a raised platform for the oak table where the higher-ranking lords and nobles usually ate.

Prince Shayan had called a meeting with Ohmaar and Zövlökh (or "Zov.")

"I thought you said you loved my father," Shayan said to Zov, the senior of the two counselors.

"I do," Zov said. "Until the day I die. But you know what I'm saying isn't coming from nowhere. We've all seen how his behavior has changed. He's going mad."

"And what should I do? Yank the crown off my father's head and declare myself the new king?"

"There is no protocol for this. It's true." Zov kept his index finger over his mouth, and it muffled him, as though the conversation were too unholy to be held aloud.

"Surely my father isn't the only king who has ever become unfit to serve," Shayan said, but it was a question.

"There was King Gheji," Ohmaar answered. He became obsessed with his pinky nail and picked at it.

"And?"

"His subjects killed him. They poisoned him."

"That obviously is not an option here."

A tear leaked from the corner of Shayan's eye, though he hadn't felt himself about to cry. This was more than he could bear. The idea of ousting his own father. The outrage this would cause. Tartaria needed strong leadership more than ever. Winning the Great War didn't mean their work was done. Not even close.

As with Burnya, Tartaria was once part of Cathyrnee, but its settlers had left decades ago to form their own kingdom. The arrival of the Sünsü had caused a momentous surge in knowledge, though not for everyone. Those gifted felt the need to break away and develop a more secular government. Predictably, domain and commerce disputes followed, then war. Unable to keep up with the advancement of armor, still favoring sunblock costuming, the Cathyrnee were soundly defeated.

At first, the Tartarian public had embraced the Great War with fervor, but not an open-ended effort to repair a decimated enemy. The war had cost taxpayers several times more than planned. This created little interest in pouring even more money into people they'd just defeated, no matter how strategic. Regardless, Prince Shayan believed it had to be done. An unstable Cathyrnee would only bring more conflict later. Besides, what was to keep the yelkin from moving northward after devouring every last Cathyrnee?

All in all, it was a catastrophic time for the King of Tartaria to lose his mind.

"I am meeting with Chief Arlyn tomorrow," Shayan said to the counselors. "Maybe that will buy us some time."

"Your father knows you're still doing this?" Zov asked him.

"I'm not clear on what he knows about anything. I just need to reassure Chief Arlyn that we haven't forgotten about them."

Zov coughed. "But, Your Highness, your father still calls for them to be considered enemies."

"I'm aware of that."

Zov sat forward. He placed his elbows on the table and stared intently at his hands, at his fingers joining to make a tent. "We might have to come up with a solution that's terminal."

"Kill my father?"

"No, no, no, I would never suggest that."

"'A solution that's *terminal*?'"

"My prince…" Zov rose from his chair and went to the nearest window. He appeared not to like whatever he saw out there, and he retreated into the Hall. "What else are we going to do?"

"How would we do it? Tell me."

"Extract from the root of an aconite plant. That would be the quickest."

Prince Shayan rubbed his forehead. "Where do we get such a plant?"

Zov shrugged. "Couldn't be too hard. There are ways."

"Think about what you're suggesting!" Ohmaar bellowed. He covered his face with his hands.

Shayan went to where Zov stood and faced him, their noses nearly touching. "Who would do it?" the prince asked the council member. "Who would give him the poison?"

Ohmaar placed his hands over his ears and bent over. "I will not be a part of this!"

"Ohmaar, my dear, we are only talking." Zov's last words were cut short by the tip of Shayan's sword puncturing his stomach. Dark blood cascaded to the floor, splashing. Zov looked down in dismay at his fatal injury. He slumped forward, lifeless, though still held up by Shayan's sword. The prince released his grip on the handle, and the deceased council member fell onto the rug.

Ohmaar sat with his mouth agape, eyes bulging with shock.

Shayan removed the sword from the bleeding body. He sheathed his sword without wiping it and remained standing over Zov's corpse. The tip of his sword dripped through its sheath. "Where did we even find this man?" the prince asked.

"His father was an advisor to your father. And his father before him. Same as me. I dare say you've behaved hastily, Your Highness."

"Maybe. I don't care. I'm glad he's dead."

"Your father might be losing his mind, but even *he* never ran a sword through someone inside this castle."

"I guess that must mean I'm not my father."

Prince Shayan gave Ohmaar a glowering stare until the former dropped his eyes. "You have done the right thing." Ohmaar's voice came low and shaky. "I can't even imagine what Zov was thinking to suggest something like that. Your sword was the only justice needed."

A quick knock at the door jarred both men. Anxious for the diversion, Ohmaar rushed to the door and opened it. Shayan watched as the advisor was handed a scroll from someone unseen in the hallway. Ohmaar untied the scroll and read it. Shayan noticed the man's hands trembling. Ohmaar clamped a hand over his mouth as if to keep from vomiting. He looked at the prince.

"What is it, Ohmaar? Speak."

"Your sister has been kidnapped."

3

SARNA

The impossible happened—she nodded off, perhaps underestimating how exhausting getting kidnapped could be. Sarna wasn't sure how much time had passed, but it was still dark. She lay on her stomach, feeling the damp ground against her cheek and the chill air on her back. She wanted to raise her head and look around but feared what she might see.

How could she have fallen asleep at a time like this? She remembered lying down while holding Lalya's hand, worried that if she didn't, she might vanish. How much longer before the inevitable happened?

She heard an ensemble of snoring from the fatigued bandits. Some snoring resembled a raspy buzz, while others came out as rhythmic snorts and wheezes. There was also quiet, whistle-like snoring and deep, rumbling snoring. She was surrounded.

Above the ambient hum of crickets, she next heard an eerie screech, followed by maniacal laughter, from somewhere far off. She believed it was a person in distress until a series of hoots revealed it was an owl. There were also rummaging noises, which she hoped were from raccoons or rodents rather than anything predatory.

However, from all these disturbances, it was a gentle wind moving through the trees that prompted her to finally lift her head. She saw that Lalya lay facing her. The poor thing was either asleep or pretending to be. Sarna thought of shaking her to find out but reconsidered when she noticed the bandit's leader lying only a couple of yards away. Luca didn't snore at all. He didn't even appear to be breathing.

Beyond him, what was left of their bonfire crackled and spat. Moving slowly, Sarna turned onto her back. The flames tossed wavering, orange-tinged shadows across the tree branches above. She stared up at the night sky. *Very well then*, she told herself, *how exactly do you plan on getting out of this particular mess?*

How indeed. There had to be a way. Some unexpected, unchaperoned moment. Was this that moment?

She wondered what would happen if she quietly found her feet and made a run for it. Without question, there would be a gang of men on her within seconds, motivated by the excuse they had been waiting for. But if the time to run away wasn't now, then when? Even if she did manage to escape, where would she go exactly?

Somewhere inside her head, she heard the furious scolding she was in for. Her parents would never forgive her for allowing this to happen. Doubtlessly and forever, this ordeal would be framed as being mostly her own fault. After all, she was the one who had promised the school it would be fine. Now look where she was. Despite lectures her entire life that there were people who would gladly hurt her if given half a chance, she was on the verge of getting gladly hurt. She'd just never truly believed it. Horrible events only happened in fairy tales with a lesson at the end, but this didn't feel like much of a fairy tale. The lesson was too obvious. Too stupid.

She tried to think of what her brother would do in this situation. Shayan wouldn't panic or beg. He would accept food and water from his captors to maintain his strength. He would leave a trail, such as clothing threads or jewelry. He would memorize every turn they took and how far they traveled.

Unfortunately, she had no means for tearing off any part of her tunic. Not wanting to call attention to herself, she hadn't worn jewelry. She'd been too shocked and disoriented to pay much attention to where they were going. Still, she knew her brother would poke and pry until he located an advantage, any advantage, no matter how small. But what possible advantage did she have?

Luca.

He was the only one protecting them. She couldn't even think about what would've happened to them already if not for him. He was it—the one advantage. She would get to know him. Learn what she could from him. She would study these men and their way of life. She could even get them to see that she wasn't so different.

She checked Lalya again. As if feeling her eyes on her, Lalya's eyes popped open and locked on hers. Lalya's lips parted as if she meant to speak, but Sarna brought a finger to her lips. Lalya's eyes widened—Lalya, who probably regretted being her friend now. Probably regretted ever meeting her. The daughter of a nobleman, she was the only person her own age that Sarna had managed to form a deep bond with, someone with whom she could share personal secrets and vulnerable thoughts. And wasn't this the root of all friendships? This search for sameness, to comfort and help navigate the challenges of growing up?

Sarna felt immensely grateful that her friend was here with her. At least she wasn't going through this alone. Even Lalya's persistent terror made Sarna feel brave in comparison. Pathetic as that was, it helped, and she needed every shred of comfort and strength she could find.

She rose onto her elbow and saw the random arrangement of sleeping bodies on the ground, highlighted by the fire, which she could now see was burning much stronger than she expected. On the far side of their camp, she noticed one of the outlaws seated on a large soapstone. Or was that a stump? He was too far away to tell. But what she *could* tell was that he was staring directly at her. He squinted while chewing on something. She considered that maybe the dancing light of the fire was deceiving her, but the more she looked, the more certain she became that his eyes were locked on her and nowhere else. Sarna shivered. She realized that he'd been watching her this entire time, as instructed. And here she'd been, foolishly believing this might be her moment to escape.

Sarna told herself it was all right. She would be patient. She would wait. She would get Luca onto her side as much as possible. Ask questions and pay attention. Learn, then learn some more. She would find the right time. It would show itself sooner or later. And when it happened, she would be ready. She would have to be.

ULAAN

She sat, praying at the only table inside her modest cottage, a portable, circular dwelling made of a lattice of flexible poles, covered with felt. Her farm was located on the outskirts of the Aimaar Forest in Burnya. As she did every morning, she recited the same three Ghe-sui mantras in her head, which always placed her mind into a peaceful trance.

Her dog Noknok sat nearby, head bowed as he feasted on table scraps. He was a Bankhar dog, a star-shaped spot on his side, historically the only breed in Jyn, now very rare. Bankhar were a breed of dog shaped through many years of cohabitation with humans and their need for a livestock guardian.

Ulaan lived on this farm, which her father had passed down to her. (Her mother had died when she was young from an unknown illness.) Ulaan grew corn, wheat, barley, and potatoes. She also raised sheep, goats, cattle, and pigs. She raised them primarily for their meat, although her goats were good for their hair. She used the hair to make the clothing she sold at her village's street market.

"*Om mani padme hum*," she chanted in a low drawl. It was the Ghe-sui prayer of compassion, the most frequently used of all their mantras.

Ulaan witnessed a series of shadows move across the window nearest her front door, imprinted against the morning light. She heard the knock and knew already it was Queen Saraal of Burnya. Ulaan went to the door, opened it, and was greeted by the sight of the Burnyan Queen, her face hidden by a headscarf, as always. Though there were no border policies between the Three Kingdoms, the Queen still preferred traveling in disguise to avoid gossip.

Ulaan bowed as Queen Saraal entered her humble home.

"No, please," the Queen said to her. "No bowing. I detest being bowed to."

The Queen gently allowed her hood to slide back off her head before unwrapping her headscarf. Behind her followed a trio of ladies-in-waiting, personal assistants, and high-ranking noblewomen who always traveled with the Queen. A dozen knights tied their horses to a cluster of oak trees, but remained outside, forming a circle around the cottage for the Queen's protection.

Noknok began to bark, excited and nervous from so much new company. This forced Ulaan to hurriedly usher the dog outside. "My Queen," Ulaan kept saying, "I'm so sorry. So sorry."

"Not to worry. I love animals," Queen Saraal said. "I do." She kissed Ulaan's cheek upon her return.

After all this time, it was still difficult for Ulaan to digest that the Queen of the entire kingdom of Burnya would ever bother to visit her filthy, modest farm, much less do so repeatedly. Ulaan often suggested visiting Queen Saraal at her castle instead, but she would always decline. The Queen feared the scandal which might erupt should subjects or family members realize she so frequently sought the counsel of a soothsayer. Though the Ghe-sui were widely respected, some viewed them as diabolical and untrustworthy. Tricksters and gypsies who claimed to be sorcerers but actually sought easy money from short-sighted fools.

Of course, the Queen paid Ulaan handsomely. Ulaan would give this money over to the Ghe-sui Temple, where her Master, the Magshaa, lived with his closest disciples. This helped Ulaan with her status, which she wasn't ashamed to admit she valued.

"May I offer you some tea, my Queen?"

"Thank you, but I won't have time. I have something very important, very urgent I need to know from you, Ulaan."

"I'll put together the chairs. Sit, please, sit."

She was already gathering a set of squirrel-fur saucer chairs for the women. She had just enough. The women formed a semicircle behind the Queen and sat mute, their hands folded inside their laps.

"How may I serve thee?" Ulaan asked. She made sure to keep her head sufficiently bowed, despite what the Queen had requested.

Queen Saraal used her scarf for dabbing her forehead dry. "I think…yes, I might be pregnant. It…it feels for real this time. Can you tell me? Can you? I must know."

Ulaan went to another room and returned with a bowl containing forty-one dried sheep droppings, along with forty-one beans and stones, laying each on a cloth which she had already spread on the floor. She touched each item to her forehead, one by one, opening her third eye and allowing intuitive perceptions to flow in.

She next divided the stones into three piles and removed four pebbles from each pile until one pebble remained. These were placed onto a nine-square grid she kept drawn on her floor with a chalky rock. The piles were separated and resorted. This resulted in a single stone inside each square, correlating to one of nature's four elements: one to fire, two to water, three to wind, four to earth.

Ulaan retook her chair in front of the Queen and shut her eyes. She leaned forward and held the Queen's wrists, turned her hands upward. Ulaan chanted a Ghe-sui mantra meant for ridding her vision of all obstacles. She fell into a trance in which every bodily function entered her consciousness—heartbeat, blood pressure, digestion, body temperature. She made her body as rigid as she could, vividly experiencing lightness, then floating. From a vantage point near the ceiling, Ulaan saw the Queen's belly glow through her robe until it lit the room. Ulaan could see a barely formed fetus inside, but the fetus vanished, snuffed out.

"No, my Queen," she said.

Queen Saraal looked up, her brow line disappearing beneath her hair. "I don't—no?"

"You are not with child."

"Are you sure?"

"I can see a child. It is no bigger than my hand. And I can hear its heartbeat. But it is not yours. I am sorry."

The Queen sat forward even further. Her maidens were no longer bowing. Ulaan had their full attention as well. "A child? Whose?" The Queen's voice rose, inflated from creeping hysteria. Outside, Noknok began barking again. She heard the knights talking to him jovially as they attempted to put the dog at ease.

Ulaan understood how crucial it was for the Queen to give an heir to her king. The entire kingdom of

Burnya had been in perpetual suspense over whether their Queen would ever provide a son. She had been pregnant twice before but had yet to make it to full term.

A fifth female appeared in the room, a younger woman formed from a gelatinous mist, which startled Ulaan. With smoky, sloping eyes filling up most of her thin, high-cheeked face, the woman appeared exceptionally beautiful…Full lips, a dimpled chin, olive skin, twin sheets of black hair…She wore an emerald-green linen chemise belted at the waist. She seemed aware of no one else in the room, not even Ulaan. A pulsing red glow within an inky cloud-like aura emanated from her womb. This was the baby! The young woman evaporated almost as quickly as she'd appeared, and Ulaan realized the Queen was saying her name without Ulaan responding. She opened her eyes.

"What is it?" the Queen was asking. "Did you see something else? You saw something else, didn't you?"

It must have been all over Ulaan's face. The young, beautiful girl had appeared to her without warning.

"Yes," Ulaan said. "I saw a girl."

"My child, maybe? I'm having a girl?"

Ulaan stood, holding her head as if not doing so would mean losing it. Thoughts arrived too rapidly, too strongly. She tried to see more, but her strength was already depleted. Visions such as these required loads of life energy. The Ghe-sui had to be careful not to use the Sünsü too much. It was a power that took what it gave, using the soul as an energy reserve. It could get worn down.

"N-no," Ulaan said, disoriented. "You're not pregnant."

The Queen was normally empathetic when Ulaan's visions left her, but not this morning. "But I must know!" Her face twisted into an anguished mask. "Ulaan, dear, look harder! Am I having a girl or a boy? This means everything!"

"This other woman I saw. A girl. She carries the king's seed. Not you."

"King Montrose has impregnated someone else?"

"The king has a mistress, my Queen. I don't know how else to tell you."

"What's her name?"

"She did not speak it."

"Does she have black hair? Dark skin? Huge eyes?"

"I believe so."

Queen Saraal got to her feet and paced the cottage. Her fingers plunged inside her hair as if meaning to yank out every strand. Her maidens sat glued to their chairs and watched her, their mouths open. Their Queen was upset, and they were, therefore, by duty and definition, failing her. Ulaan could sense they resented her more than ever now for her influence.

The Queen left Ulaan's cottage without saying another word. Her maidens gave each other a puzzled look before dashing after her like baby chicks realizing their mother had flown off without them.

Ulaan stood there, stunned. She listened to the rustling of chainmail and leather outside as the knights and maidens swarmed into formation to leave. After they were long gone, she stayed standing there, even after Noknok scratched at the front door to be let in. She cringed to think of the spectacle she'd just set into motion. Even worse, the Queen had forgotten to pay her, a common occurrence when people were told what they didn't want to hear. Even the Queen.

SARNA

The bandits sat around a fire, eating roasted squirrels. Sarna tried a bite because she was starving. The taste was somewhere between chicken and rabbit with a nutty aftertaste, likely from the squirrel's diet.

As planned, she had been learning a lot since being kidnapped. For instance, she learned that the forest was teeming with edible wildlife. If necessary, she could eat insects, except for spiders and millipedes. If a bug owned a crunchy, chitinous exoskeleton, such as ants or crickets, they were food.

"You can also eat worms," Luca told her. He sat on her right, next to a bonfire. "Capturing animals or catching fish is hard and takes time, but it's always easy to find insects. Just kick over a rock."

He warned her to always stay away from any brightly colored creature. This went for plants and amphibians, too—if something carried flashy colors, it was nature's way of letting you know it was poisonous.

Sarna learned it was always best to cook what you ate. That way, it required less energy to digest. For the bandits, surviving the wild was a constant balance of hunting, foraging, and saving energy.

Lalya sat by the fire on Sarna's right. She refused to eat, choosing instead to gaze into the flames as if wishing to jump in. Sarna knew, as Lalya likely did, that it was only a matter of time before they were assaulted. The bandits wouldn't stop talking about it. Luca was holding them off as best he could, but soon the bandits' collective, primordial desire for carnal release would overtake their respect for his leadership.

It didn't take long for Sarna to discern that Luca was the only bandit with any semblance of sense or wit about him. She couldn't take her eyes off him. She wasn't attracted to him in the least, but there was a defiant bravery about him. She still wanted to get to know him better. Find out exactly who her captor was. At least find some leverage for prolonging her and Lalya's survival.

She could see that Luca cared for these men, these fellow ex-soldiers who had done their duty by fighting for her father, only to be discarded once their use was finished. Many of them still carried battle scars, even Luca, who wore a Y-shaped scar on his cheek. She hadn't noticed it until seeing him closer.

He caught her looking at him and grinned. "Enjoying your first taste of squirrel, Your Highness?"

"Not especially."

"I don't imagine it compares to what you're used to. My apologies for that, Your Highness."

"Stop calling me that."

"What should I call you?"

She ignored the question. "Have you heard from my father yet?"

"Have you seen our messenger return?"

"No."

"Then I haven't heard from your father yet. Probably tomorrow morning. Not to worry, though, your High—um, Princess. I'll get you safely back to your daddy before you know it."

"Were you a soldier?"

"You know I was."

Sarna looked around the fire at the other men, their grim, dirty faces cast in orange. Some prepared for sleep while others talked and drank. A few emerged from the forest carrying more wood for the waning flames. Several sentries changed shifts.

"I can tell you're having a hard time with these men," she said.

"They've been through a lot. Besides, they love me in their own way. I'm loved by everyone. Maybe you will, too, Princess. Before you know it."

"Just let us live, please."

One of the men approached, and Sarna heard Lalya's breath catch. The bandit bent down and squatted. His grin exhibited several missing teeth. When it became evident this was all the man intended to do, Sarna relaxed. Yes, they would definitely be sleeping near Luca again tonight.

"If it counts for anything," Sarna told Luca, "I meant what I said earlier. I do feel for all of you. For what you've been through. It's not right what my father did. I question much of what he does."

Luca nodded, but his expression gave away nothing. The squatting man reached out to touch Lalya, and she scooted away. She whimpered as she took Sarna's arm.

"Hermonus!" Luca said to the man. "Easy. They're worth a lot of money. We can't go spoiling them."

"Not even this one? Who cares about her?" He reached again for Lalya.

Sarna slapped his hand away. "Stop!"

The man recoiled and fell over. He kicked to get further away. At first, Sarna thought this was meant to mock her, except his reaction appeared too genuine. He was truly injured, as though her touch had burned him. Wild with dismay, the man got to his feet and rushed to the other side of the fire. He held the spot where she'd touched him and grimaced.

Luca thought this was uproarious. "What did you do to him?" he asked, still laughing.

"Lalya is every bit as valuable as I am," Sarna said. "No one is to touch her. No one."

He made that sloppy, sideways grin of his. "Better sleep close to me then." He winked at her and walked off. She watched him, the way he strolled as if feeling so great, the way he moved his body, even the way he *didn't* move his body. There was a rugged handsomeness about him. His hazel eyes crinkled at the corners when he smiled.

Realizing they were alone, Sarna took Lalya's hand, and they shared a distressed look around them. Both girls sprang to their feet to follow Luca.

CHIEF ARLYN

He rode horseback, accompanied by what was left of his people. These included women, children, warriors, bodyguards, and servants. He no longer kept up with how far they had traveled. Though he'd been too exhausted to make a headcount yet, it appeared there couldn't have been more than a thousand Cathyrnee left. Twenty of them made a barrier around him and the Chieftess, all riding horses, traveling across the Orgoon Plains. An additional thirty horses allowed them to switch to a fresh mount as needed. They possessed few other animals anymore.

They made it to the grasslands of Dresda and headed towards the southern range of the Zavgüi Mountains. No matter how many scouts Chief Arlyn employed to gain warning, no matter what defensive maneuvers they attempted, they were always overrun within seconds. They had held off the yelkin attack the previous night, but not before most of his remaining people were slaughtered. If the yelkin had wanted, they could've massacred every one of them. The only saving grace for the Cathyrnee was their numbers. The yelkin would simply tire from their rampage, their bellies overfilled.

Chief Arlyn carried several deep cuts across his arms and shoulders from where he had fended off the creatures from his wife. A quilt of seeping bandages crisscrossed his body. He managed the excruciating pain by drinking babsulisk juice, a nectar from a superfruit native to Jyn.

Chieftess Yarlaa rode beside him, unharmed, wearing her red battle helmet. She had eluded injury by crawling beneath their bed.

Arlyn had never wanted to abandon their lands, but they were left with no choice. Their last means of defense was to become mobile. He'd sent a Shuudan Rider to Tartaria to inform King Khilji and Prince Shayan of their worsening situation. Arlyn hoped they could still somehow arrange a meeting to discuss the terms under which they could acquire help against the yelkin. At least loan them some builders to construct protective walls.

Asking his enemies for aid was a major wound to Chief Arlyn's pride, something he thought he would never do. However, his days were now filled with actions he thought he would never do.

A Ghe-Sui shaman named Corsika rode on the other side of Yarlaa. Corsika was a thin strand of a woman with blue hair. She was so small that she seemed to barely even be there. Though some Ghe-sui stayed with the Cathyrnee after the formation of Burnya, it was uncommon for anyone to have their own personal shaman. But the two women shared a bond, which Arlyn tolerated, if for no other reason than to make his wife feel safer. Arlyn personally considered the Ghe-sui fraudsters. If they genuinely possessed special powers, he had certainly never witnessed it. Where were her powers against the yelkin?

No sooner was this thought inside his head than it escaped his mouth. Yarlaa stared straight ahead, too drained from lack of sleep and excessive trauma to interfere.

When Corsika didn't answer, Arlyn repeated: "Where were your powers last night? We could've used them."

"I did what I could, Chief Arlyn. I battled two of them. The yelkin are not easy to kill."

Yarlaa removed her battle helmet and turned to her husband. "Leave her alone," she told him. "Now is not the time for blame. Everyone needs each other."

Arlyn started to contradict her, but Corsika spoke up: "What has become of our people. It's hurting me as well, Chief Arlyn. Deeper than I can express."

"Isn't there anything the other Ghe-sui could do for us?" Arlyn asked her. "Isn't the Magshaa—or whatever you call him—isn't he supposed to be mighty and powerful? Couldn't he just snap his fingers and kill these things?"

Corsika adjusted herself atop her horse. "The Magshaa doesn't believe in using his powers to kill. It is not our way."

"As he's continually proven."

Corsika lowered her head, shamed. She was likely all too aware of the frustrations people had with her leader. So much supposed power but never willing to use it.

They believed that the blessings of the Sünsü, a spiritual enchantment which had befallen the Realm of Jyn only three centuries ago, were intended only for benevolence. It was an event that accelerated the advancement of their race from a primitive age of stone and sticks to one of metal and steel, otherwise known as the "Great Awakening." To this day, however, no one fully understood this magic, not even its master, the Magshaa.

Arlyn checked over his shoulder at the wide trail of people on foot behind them, stretching away as far as the eye could see. Dotted throughout the masses were the occasional carriage or cart, some holding grains or rice, others carrying wounded. The midday sun bore down on them, practically baking them. When a breeze would move through the plains, Arlyn could sense the relief wash over his people. Could hear their sighs. He knew he had to do something, no matter how extreme the measure. Before long, they would run out of food. Sickness and starvation would take hold. There were other formidable predators about besides only the yelkin.

"I do know someone who might help us," Corsika said while looking off, as if searching the horizon for whom she spoke of. "Actually, I think they would be *glad* to help."

"And you're only mentioning them now?"

This brought another scornful glance from Chieftess Yarlaa. Arlyn couldn't help it, though. His patience was dissipating.

"The Dark Shulam," Corsika said.

"*Dark?* Why are they 'dark'?"

"They're shamans who were once part of the Ghesui, but they branched off and formed their own practice. They grew angry that the Magshaa wouldn't share more of his power."

"I like them already."

"They live in covens at the base of the Zavgüi Mountains now," Corsika said. "They study the Sünsü as best they can. Whereas the Magshaa is protective of his powers, the Dark Shulam look for any excuse to use theirs." Corsika paused. She seemed to await a response from Chief Arlyn. When she appeared confident that Arlyn was fully listening, she continued, "We could seek them out. I could astral project and call a meeting with them."

"*Astral project*, huh? And what's the drawback?"

"They're not going to help us without getting something in return. What that 'something' might be is worrisome."

"In what way?"

"All they care about is power. Also, their appearance is quite frightening. Without the guidance of the Magshaa, they've become immoral and wicked, and it shows on them."

"And this is why they're 'dark?'"

"It validates their rebellion, I suppose."

Arlyn thought for a moment. "I've sent a messenger ahead to King Khilji of Tartaria," he said. "I'm meeting with his son, Prince Shayan. Let's see how that goes. Don't know if I'm quite ready for witches and wizards yet."

He gave Corsika a look that sought confirmation. She met his eyes. The Ghe-sui shaman smiled thinly and nodded.

Chief Arlyn jerked on his horse's reins. This was the animal's cue to reverse course. Arlyn galloped back through his people to perform a wellness check. He would occasionally dismount to talk to someone who seemed in special need of encouragement or comfort. He checked on the wounded. The human drone of chatter and moaning rumbled on around him.

KING MONTROSE

The King of Burnya lifted the nude maiden onto his lap. She sat facing him and wrapped her legs around his waist. He pressed his bearded face between her breasts and inhaled her cinnamon scent.

Montrose copulated with her in a field of plush carpeting and fringe-traced, velvet pillows the size of baby elephants. To add to the surrealness, flamingos and peacocks tiptoed about the room but remained, for the most part, closest to the walls. More nude bodies crawled over one another nearby, stretching, reaching, touching, probing. This was the king taking full advantage of the Queen being away on yet another expedition to consult her shaman. Her absence made for the perfect occasion to have an orgy. To imbibe obscene amounts of babsulisk.

The general populace of Burnya remained unaware of such events, though there were rumors. Admired for his charm, King Montrose was better known for his drunkenness, wasteful spending, and scandalous sex life. Still, many adored him for having kept Burnya out of the Great War between Tartaria and the Cathyrnee. (Burnya had once been part of Cathyrnee but separated long ago to practice their own religion, a monotheistic faith in contrast to the polytheism practiced by the Cathyrnee.) Besides, King Montrose had given raises to his military and canceled unpopular taxes. So, behind closed doors, they let him do whatever he wanted.

Nearing climax, King Montrose felt a tapping on his shoulder. He looked up to see Artemis the Gold Master, who stood there, frowning.

"My Lord, I do so profusely apologize for interrupting."

"Then, by the gods, why would you dare?"

A second nude girl knelt beside the king. This was his favorite mistress—Ozyan. Her beauty was so profound that her mere entrance into a room could guillotine all conversation. King Montrose was obsessed with her.

"I need to talk with you as well," Ozyan said to him, though much more sweetly than Artemis had.

"I would never disrespect you, My Lord," Artemis said, undeterred. "I'm just wondering if we could chat for a moment. Alone. It's that important."

"Chat with me right now. I have no secrets."

"Don't ignore me!" Ozyan pouted.

The other girl kept riding the king as though no one else were there. She gasped louder with each bounce of her waist, making a performance of it.

"I am aware of the complex absurdity of my timing," Artemis said, "but I can't seem to catch you anywhere else anymore."

"So stop trying to catch me. Go away forever, Artemis. Or I will have you killed."

"Yes, yes, yes, I would love to go away. But there are some matters I need to discuss with you. Matters that can no longer wait. Not another second."

"Like what?"

"The refugee situation, for instance? We have hundreds of Cathyrnee showing up at our gates every day."

"This is exactly *not* the sort of thing you should risk interrupting me with." King Montrose clutched onto the maiden's shoulder and moved with her. "Those are ongoing problems you're talking about."

"But this wide-open immigration policy. These sex parties. The parades. The tax exemptions. The life-sized golden statue you had made of yourself? My Lord, I do appreciate that you're a great patron of the arts and humanity, but this level of spending is simply unsustainable."

King Montrose reached out and touched Ozyan's left side. He rubbed his thumb over her breast, and she pressed herself against his hand.

"Figure something out then," said Montrose to his Gold Master. "Isn't that your job?"

"Right, but you're the king, and you're making all of these huge financial decisions without consulting me. There's only—"

"Artemis, one more word, and I'll have you executed. So bless the gods, I mean it."

The Gold Master didn't flinch as Montrose was liable to threaten anyone's life multiple times throughout the day. "My Lord, if we don't start paying attention to this kingdom's economy, you might as well execute *everyone*."

This got the king's attention. He went still. The girl atop the king ceased her bouncing and looked at Artemis, too. Montrose patted Artemis on his arm. "You're right, you're right. I'm sorry."

Artemis started to express his relief but was cut off by the king looking into the doe-like eyes of his main mistress, Ozyan. He laid his hand around her neck, then guided her head towards the other girl. Ozyan hesitated before appearing to get the hint. She laid her own hand around the other girl's neck and pulled her in. Her lips closed around hers while her other hand trailed downwards.

"This is my last orgy for a while," said the King of Burnya. "I promise. Probably."

Artemis remained standing there, mesmerized. "I understand, My Lord. I will come back later."

"And Artemis? I know what I'm doing, all right? I'm the king."

"That you are, My Lord," Artemis muttered, his attention now frozen on what the two girls were doing to each other. "All hail."

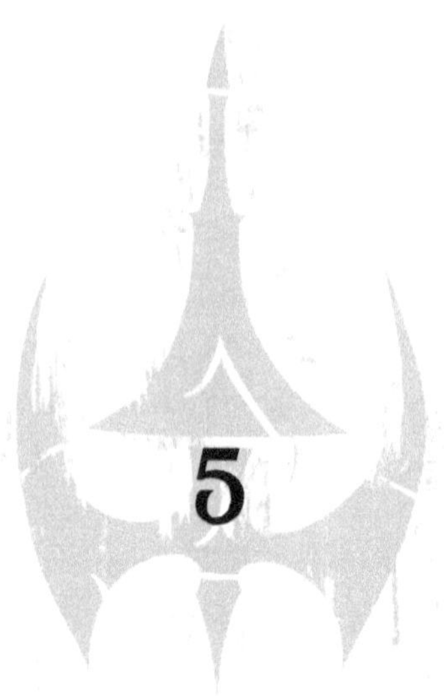

5

ULAAN

The horses screamed from being on fire. They tried fleeing from their own haunches as they became chewed with flames. A vast army of shadow people chased them, swords drawn, their red eyes like smoldering embers, all chanting in a language Ulaan could not understand. On a hill overlooking the carnage stood a pale child who whispered. She tried to understand what the child was saying but could not make out the words. When the child's voice grew louder, she could tell the child was a boy.

The sky was a canvas of honey swished with blood. The ribbon-like bodies of three flying drakksuks threaded a bank of heavy, gray clouds, which flashed and surged with lightning. The drakksuk were frightening creatures with the head of a crocodile atop a serpentine body, supported by a ten-meter span of bat-like wings. Their shrieks traveled through her, rattling her organs. She pressed her hands to her ears and fell to her knees.

"I know who you are," she finally understood the boy to say, his voice now inside her mind. "I have always known you. Nobody cares about you more than I do."

The child's whisper grew into a roar as he used both hands to hold up a human head. Ulaan's screams mixed with the horses' when she saw the decapitated head was her own, her mouth carving her face open with torment.

Ulaan awoke. She sat up, sweating. She saw the morning sun through her window. A ruby-red haze hugged the horizon. She could still hear the horses screaming as they burned. Could still hear the roar of drakksuks.

It was Spring, the season of new life. Calves and goats were being born and needed looking after. After breakfast, she would go out to milk the cows, while the herder tended to the sheep. Afterward, she had gardening to do. Potatoes and corn to pick.

The grass needed cutting, then drying, then spread for food among the animals. There was water to pump for the animals as well. She had to clean the manure out of the stables and cook for the farm helpers. The work seemed endless, and Ulaan already felt weary.

She often thought of how much easier her life would be with a husband. She had a small staff of helpers, of course, but never enough. Naturally, the hired hands had no interest in a fat, aging mystic woman with a bulbous nose, flappy ears, and hips so round they caused her to waddle.

She'd had a man once—a farmer from a Burnyan village who worked with her father. Ulaan and the farmer had fallen in love after knowing each other since childhood.

"I know who you are," he'd once told her, exactly as the boy had in her dream. "I have always known you. Nobody cares about you more than I do."

They lived happily together for four years until the Great War started. Although Burnya was not involved, the Tartarian kingdom offered good money for soldiers, no matter where they were from. The farmer was swiftly killed in battle, and Ulaan was devastated. After her parents also passed away, she discovered the healing power of babsulisk. It helped her stop caring anymore.

She left the running of the ranch to the workers and became less involved. Her health deteriorated, and she was taken to a healing center run by the Ghe-sui. Every day, the shamans would visit her and consult her about the benefits of Sünsü. How she should consider learning to use this gift passed down from the gods. Turn her life around.

She ignored them. After healing, she went back to the farm where she resumed drinking and forgot about the Ghe-sui. After a few months, she noticed her memory was disappearing. She even became prone to violence. One morning, a ranchman knocked on her door, concerned about the cattle. She slapped him for no reason. Despite her drunken fog, she was shocked at herself. She was becoming a monster. That same evening, her right hand went numb. The numbness rose up her arm and throughout her entire right side. She could no longer talk.

Ulaan was taken back to the same Ghe-sui healing center. Again, the shamans prodded her to join them, claiming they saw "abilities" in her. Not everyone had them. When the Magshaa himself visited her, she recalled being astounded at how petite and feeble he appeared. So odd to think he possessed so much power! Regardless, the aura of peace and harmony that enveloped him left a profound impression on her.

With his guidance, Ulaan learned to examine her life with a sober mind: What did she have? What was life about? Why was she born? She had always felt lonely, depressed, empty, hopeless, with no sense of direction or purpose. She pleaded with the Magshaa to please help her. Teach her to be stronger. Teach her the Sünsü.

And he did, showing her the power that was within her all along. She learned no amount of money, success, entertainment, or narcotic nectar would ever fill her soul. This could only be accomplished by the love and protection of the Ghe-sui and its Master.

Though Ulaan had always possessed a heightened sensitivity to her environment, she never thought anything special of this. She had dreams that often came true, but she dismissed them easily since many concerned the insignificant or events that could likely be guessed anyway. She'd always refused to accept that she was gifted.

The Magshaa taught her to fine-tune her psychic senses, to activate her etheric and astral vision for discerning the true nature of the world, to see objects and people in faraway places, and to make sense of spontaneous visions and dreams. She learned to experience scenes from the past and understand their meaning, take a peek into the near and distant future. To establish contact with the spirit world and ask them for guidance.

Ulaan became such an adept psychic that her reputation spread, even reaching the attention of Queen Saraal of Burnya. She chose Ulaan because she didn't live at the temple, unlike most other shamans. Though the Queen traveled with a retinue, including ladies of the court, traveling to Ulaan's farm remained the more discretionary option.

Lately, the Queen had increased her visits to the extent that it became emptying for Ulaan. The Sünsü was never a sorcery to be handled lightly. As the Queen required more counseling, Ulaan could feel it fading her. Too many lines had etched into her face for someone her age. White hairs blended with her naturally darker hair. She often slept the entire day after one of the Queen's visits. It was becoming a problem.

Still shaken from her nightmare, Ulaan got up from bed and went to her front door. She opened it and allowed her lungs to infuse with the luscious morning air. Many ranchmen had arrived already, dressed in their wool hats and boots. She looked to the east and shivered from a breeze far too frosty for spring. Her senses bristled with dread, a feeling she'd had before but rarely this strong. The dream had created a heavy ambiance of doom around her.

She realized it had been months since she'd visited the Ghe-sui Temple or consulted with the Magshaa. Perhaps she was overdue. He would understand what her dream meant. They would work it out together. The Magshaa would calm her mind by once again verifying they could handle anything together. He was excellent at this.

Ulaan went back inside to dress. She later returned outside to find her head ranchman, Lomen. She informed him she was taking one of the horses to the temple. She would be back tomorrow morning. Tomorrow afternoon at the latest. She told him to take care of the farm while she was gone. Everything was fine.

SARNA

She and Lalya remained in Luca's shadow as they traveled the forest, getting murkier by the step. These bandits might not have been the best-smelling, most sophisticated men in this world, but Sarna couldn't help but admire their adeptness for wilderness survival.

Finding uncontaminated water was the most important key, the main source of which was rainwater captured in jugs. When this got used up, they dug for the water. Cattails and cottonwoods indicated nearby underground moisture, which would condense into water when they dug a deep enough hole. Like humans, plants sweated, so they tied tiny bags around leafy branches where more water accumulated. They also collected water from puddles inside rock outcroppings. They scooped from streams, always making sure to boil the water first.

During a rest, Luca showed Sarna how to tie a variety of knots. She already knew the bowline knot from sewing. He also showed her the double half-hitch, used to attach one end of a rope around an object—a useful knot for building a shelter against a tree.

She learned how to move through the wilderness undetected, to use the terrain to become invisible. The first way to do this, as Luca demonstrated, was to be soft-footed. This allowed them to feel the ground and avoid cracking twigs and sticks. They wore tight-fitting clothing to avoid getting tangled in briars, weeds, or overhanging branches. Their soft fabric soundproofed their movement. Plates of armor were worn so as not to touch each other.

When hunting, they walked in erratic patterns to

mimic the sound of other animals. If prey was found, they approached with the sun at their back, hindering their target's vision.

When the sun disappeared behind the treetops, the bandits stopped again to build a fire and eat. Sarna could not remember having felt so grateful for anything in her life. Her legs no longer contained enough starch to hold her. Lalya had fallen several times herself. Each time, Luca would grimace and help her up with Sarna on her other side. The men laughed at the first couple of falls, but then it happened so often that they stopped even noticing.

Lalya walked with small, staggering steps and hung her head. Upon noticing the group had stopped, she went abruptly to the ground and lay there, her head haloed in muddy leaves. The bandits set about cleaning and cooking some rabbits they'd killed, while others prepared the fire.

"What is your plan?" Sarna asked Luca. She had a seat on the ground next to her friend but maintained her dignity about it. "How are you going to get your ransom if we keep walking around in the woods?"

"We are not 'wandering around.' We're on a very specific path. We plan to meet your brother at Thygoras Meadows. Same place where Cathyrnee surrendered to your father. Before that, though, we're meeting up with my messenger right here."

She tried to think of something to add but couldn't. That seemed to be the end of the subject. She would be saved, and everything would be all right. Back to normal.

"Why are you looking at me like that?" Luca asked her, again, that half-grin, right brow arching like a sideways S.

"Like what?"

Luca opened his arms but was looking beyond her. "And there he is!"

Sarna turned and saw a man entering their resting spot on horseback, which meant they couldn't have been too far from a trail. The messenger was greeted warmly by the bandits. His eyes sought Luca as soon as he'd dismounted. Luca parted the men to reach the messenger, and they hugged. The messenger handed him a scroll, which Luca read. Everyone held still and watched him read.

Luca looked up from the scroll. He smiled and held his arms out. "Prince Shayan agrees to the ransom!"

A cheer went up from the bandits, some of them even embracing. Luca handed the scroll to one of the bandits, who read it aloud to the others.

Sarna scooped Lalya into her lap and held her head. "Did you hear that, Lalya? We're almost through this. Have strength."

Lalya nuzzled her nose into Sarna's leg. "Please, let it be true," she whispered. "I want to go home."

Sarna picked a few leaves from her friend's hair. It had rained last night, so their hair and clothing had matted onto them. Lalya was suffering from exposure and starvation.

She heard Luca walking back over to them. She

didn't look up because she knew the pattern of his footfalls by now.

"Your brother has agreed to pay us what we asked," he told her. "This is great news, right?"

"No tricks?" she asked him. "Take your money, then hand us over, and good-bye?"

"Worry more about your brother. We just want our money. He's the one more likely to pull a trick."

Luca handed her the scroll, and she unraveled it. It was a message to her captors that the Kingdom of Tartaria would meet their demands in exchange for the princess, granted she was completely unharmed. The scroll was signed by Prince Shayan, her brother, with the seal of the Tartarian Kingdom.

"I'm going to miss you, Princess," Luca told her.

She started to respond, but Lalya stirred and sat up. She winced and held her stomach. "Lalya comes with me," she said.

"Sorry. No, she doesn't."

"She does so!"

"Don't recall seeing her name on that scroll, Your Highness."

"You're *keeping* her?" Sarna stood to face him. "Why would you do that?"

"Because she's worth money, too. We can marry her off, sell her as a servant, or a whore. Plenty of things."

"I-I'll get you more money. Tell me what you want!"

"I think we've already milked you for what we can,

no?"

"No! I will not allow you to keep her!"

The volume and vehemence of her voice brought the other conversations to a halt. Luca noticed the attention they now had and laughed. "Is that so?" he asked her.

"She's sick. She needs medicine. Look at her!"

Lalya burst into tears. "I want to go home," she whined. "Let me go home. Princess, tell them."

Luca gazed down at his boots and appeared genuinely dejected. Sarna could sense there was a compassionate man inside of him somewhere. He didn't want to be doing this. The way he behaved in front of his men was just a shield. A false act he played to keep their respect. A role. Please, let it be a role.

"She doesn't deserve this," Sarna added.

Luca turned to one of his scouts. "Fetch me a bow and some arrows. Not those! Those are mine. Those over there. We're going to see what our princess is made of."

The scout came back with the requested bow and arrows. He wore a long beard to the center of his chest. Most of the bandits did. Sarna could see that the other bandits were gravely concerned with what was happening. Why was their leader providing a weapon to their captive?

Luca pointed. "Hit that tree," he said to Sarna, "and I'll release your friend to go with you."

"I've never shot an arrow in my life."

Luca handed her the bow and arrow. He positioned

his body behind hers. "I'll show you. Stand straight. Keep your feet apart, even with your shoulders."

Sarna tried twisting away, but he shoved her back into place.

"You can do this," he whispered. "I'll teach you. Do as I say and save your friend."

Sarna began to protest further but felt the savage strength of his arms. They enclosed her as his hands covered hers, taking control of the bow and arrow she held.

"Relax," he told her. "Relax your grip. Turn the bow horizontal and let the arrow rest facing upwards. Like this. See? There. Good."

Sarna did as he showed her. She became hyper-aware of his full body pressed against her back. His breath moved her hair when he spoke.

"Now push the nock of the arrow onto the string. Like that. Between these two nocking points. Bring the bow back and put your fingers on the string. This finger goes above the arrow. Right there. These two fingers go below it. Wait. You're holding it too hard. Relax."

She gulped and tried relaxing as he told her. She could feel everyone's eyes on them. It was hard to concentrate with him holding her from behind. A charged layer of heat developed between them, becoming hotter the longer they touched. And they kept touching. The contact would seem incidental to the archery lesson, but she had her doubts.

"Pull back the string so this finger is under your

chin," he told her. "Now look down the arrow and line it with your target. See?"

"I only have to hit the tree? Anywhere?"

"Let's aim for the knot. Careful. Come on. You're tensing up too much."

Extraordinarily hard to relax when I can feel your thighs against my rear, she wanted to say. Her knees shook.

One of the other bandits trotted over to them. He was a different scout. "A patrol's coming! They tailed our messenger!"

"A patrol?" Luca asked him. "Are you sure?"

"Tartarian Knights. I recognize their banners. They're heavily armed."

"How far away?"

"We have maybe an hour. "

Luca backed up from Sarna and spun her around. "Your brother still has patrols looking for us? And you accused *me* of planning tricks?"

"They're probably unaware of the arrangement," she said. "Just hide and let them go by."

"I'm not going to attack them," he said, monotone. "*We* are."

Luca shouted for his men to prepare an ambush. The bandits gathered up their weapons and shields. They paired off to paint each other's faces, to help blend in with the foliage. Luca wandered off and returned to Sarna with a large leaf. Cupped inside the leaf was the dye they'd made from berries and tree bark. He dipped his fingers into the pasty mix, then brought his fingers towards her face. She flinched.

"Be still!" he snapped at her. "If you're going to be a warrior, you need to look like one."

Luca used two fingers to paint multiple stripes down her cheeks. She looked into his face while he did so, noticing how much concentration he put into it, as if creating a masterpiece. Behind him, she noticed the other bandits pausing occasionally to regard them, bewildered. She could tell they were beginning to resent and distrust the attention he gave her. Worried perhaps that their leader was going soft on them.

Once done, he straightened to admire his handiwork. "There," he said. He touched her chin and steered her face around. "I've never seen someone so ready to kill."

6

KING MONTROSE

When he retired to his chambers, King Montrose found Ozyan already in his bed. She sat up, arms crossed beneath her naked breasts, her back pressed against the headboard—cushioned, padded, stitched, and styled to opulent perfection. She frowned.

The royal bedroom was luxurious, with black walls trimmed with white borders and complemented by white bedding. An enormous chandelier dangled above the bed while exotic flowers in golden, ceramic planters sat about the room. Reflecting the king and his mistress was a free-standing mirror with an engraved wooden frame bordered with detailed angelic designs.

"How did you get in here?" King Montrose asked her.

"I climbed in through the window." When he actually looked at the window, she slapped her lap and laughed. "I walked in through the door, silly! Everyone has seen me do it a thousand times."

"But you cannot be in here now, my dove. The Queen is due to return."

"Yet here I am."

"Ozyan, you're becoming much too bold."

"But I love you, My Lord. You're my everything. Don't you love me?"

"That's not the issue here."

"Is the Queen that stupid, though? She knows who you are."

"She knows about my indiscretions…to a point. She does not know about *you*."

"Stop talking. Make love to me, My Lord."

Montrose kicked off his slippers and disrobed. "We must make this fast, though. She would go completely mad at seeing you in her bed like this."

"You sound like you're afraid of her."

The king stood wearing only a loincloth, barely visible beneath his extensive belly. "That's because I *am* afraid of her, my dove. The Queen is very popular."

"But so are you! The Kingdom of Burnya adores you! Look how rich you've made this kingdom."

He bent over and dropped his loincloth. He stood and stepped out of them. He noticed a nightstand holding a goblet and lifted the goblet. He found it still contained a few gulps of babsulisk, which he tossed down his throat.

"I cannot wait to be your Queen one day." Ozyan

swept the covers over, an invitation for the king to climb in. "But I assume this is the part where you tell me to be patient again?"

"You have to be patient. It will happen." He bounded into bed beside her. He took her lithe body in his arms and squeezed her. He reached a hand around to caress the pleasingly pliable flesh of her backside. "You are the most beautiful, the most—most ravishing woman in all of Burnya."

She grabbed his cock while throwing a soft, brown leg over his waist. "Not forever, I won't be. Wait too long to make me your Queen, and you're not going to want me anymore."

"Impossible."

"Then how can it be done? Tell me. How will you ever get rid of her?"

Montrose lowered his head and kissed the nape of Ozyan's neck. She stroked the back of his head. She made a gratified noise and scratched her nose.

Yes, how exactly did he plan on getting rid of the Queen? Queen Saraal wasn't old enough for him to simply await a natural death. There was the dilemma of her not providing an heir yet, but this wasn't enough to *divorce* her. Burnya *loved* her. The Queen was a leader who stood with her people, not above them. She wouldn't even tolerate her subjects bowing to her! She used numerous charities to champion underdogs, making herself an emblem of humility and grace. There was no chance of making this delicious nymph his Queen without suffering the ire of the entire kingdom. King Montrose had simply promised Ozyan the title in a cross-eyed, drunken, lust-driven stupor, only to now be reminded of the promise daily.

Montrose brought Ozyan onto him because he was too heavy to lie on her. He pushed inside, and she gasped, her tiny, plump mouth opening, her lips sticking at the corners. Those lips, this face, that body. He would do anything to keep her. She was a goddess to him, but low-born to the rest. His kingdom would never tolerate marriage to a village girl. He just couldn't decide if he cared. Right now, he decided to care only about those slender legs squeezing his lower back. She yelped from the ecstasy of their movement together until she became so loud, he was forced to press a hand over her mouth. To silence her.

SHAYAN

The prince visited his mother, Queen Abika, in her private quarters. He found her sitting at her vanity desk, accompanied by blue-and-gold silk-upholstered furniture and malachite candelabras. A gilded piano sat across the room, which only Sarna knew how to partially play. Over a stone fireplace hung a pristine portrait of the family.

Shayan noticed the mostly empty bottle of babsulisk in his mother's left hand. "You're drinking too much of that stuff. Every time I see you now."

"The king's advisor is missing."

"Which one?"

"Zov. Have you seen him?"

"I have not. I'm surprised anyone even noticed him missing. Those counselors are useless."

Queen Abika ran a brush through her hair, then seemed to lose interest after a single stroke. "Why must you be the one to deliver her ransom?" she asked her son. "Why can't you send someone else?"

"Because they requested me specifically. They want to humiliate us, which is fine. I need to make sure this is done right anyway."

"When?"

"Now. Just came to tell you farewell. My knights are waiting for me downstairs."

"Why not wait for a patrol to find them?"

"Because Sarna could get hurt. Any patrol I find, I'm sending them home."

"Bring your sister back safe to us. Give them whatever they want. Don't be a hero." Queen Abika pushed herself to her feet and stumbled over to the window. It was a casement window which she opened to the side. She extended her arm and poured out the rest of her bottle. She looked back at her son, sneering at him. "Happy?"

Shayan heard shouting from outside the window. The contents of her bottle had evidently doused someone. Maybe several people. The Queen returned to her seat at the vanity, oblivious.

"Wish me luck," he told her.

"We're going to have a full inquiry into why your sister was traipsing through the woods with so little protection. Who approved of that?"

"I don't believe anyone did, Mother."

"I would also like to know why it took so long for us to find out. Why did no one tell us?"

"Fear of blame or punishment, I'd assume. Father would have anyone even remotely involved put to death."

"Not necessarily. He's been known to reward those who help."

"Then perhaps we're a lot more isolated in this castle than we care to admit."

"Does the king even know?"

"I've done my best to keep it a secret so far. From everyone. I even delayed my meeting with Chief Arlyn and didn't tell him why."

"How did he take it?"

"No idea. I imagine he's insulted."

"Who cares? Let word out that the princess was successfully kidnapped for ransom, and we'll have every criminal in all of Jyn looking to snatch her. She'll never leave my sight again."

The prince nodded.

The door creaked open, and King Khilji entered, completely nude, walking with the aid of a wooden staff Shayan had never seen before. Dropping the staff, the king spread his arms wide.

"I am naked!" he announced.

"Father?" Shayan asked him, his own voice sounding small and helpless, child-like.

"Gods help us," Queen Abika muttered.

"I am naked!" King Khilji reaffirmed.

"Where are your clothes?" the Queen shrieked at her husband.

"Naked!"

"I'm off then," Shayan said. His path to leave became blocked by the king. "Father, I have to leave for something quite important. Allow me to pass."

"This is me," King Khilji told his son. "The *real* me."

Shayan attempted once more to leave the chambers, but his father refused to move. "Father," the prince said, "it's important!"

"Important?" King Khilji asked. "What's so important? Something I should know about?"

The prince kissed the king on the cheek, then pried his way past him, even having to shoulder-nudge him out of the way. In the hall, Shayan paused a moment to lean his head against the wall. He pressed his fist to his mouth and fought to keep his emotions under control.

A trio of female servants came walking up the hallway and stopped short upon seeing their prince with his head against the wall. Prince Shayan wiped his eyes and rushed by them.

"Does the king need us?" one called to his back.

"Go right in," Shayan said, but without turning around, still walking on his way to rescue his sister, the princess. He smiled when he heard the girls yelping, aghast at the sight of their naked king.

7

SARNA

She watched as Luca and his men set their ambush, maintaining noise discipline as they surrounded the trail. Soon, the order of Tartarian knights trotted their horses into view. Two scouts rode at the front, scanning the foliage for danger.

As before, the plan was for Luca to shoot an arrow first. This would signal the rest to charge with swords and axes drawn, attacking relentlessly until Luca gave the word to stop. He made sure each man knew their role, so when the assault began, there would be no need to call out commands.

Naturally, the ambush would be somewhat modified, since it was against trained, heavily armored fighters rather than a female art class. They hoped to hit the knights hard and fast enough to disorient them, then flee before they could muster reinforcements. The last thing the bandits wanted was for their ambush to become a lengthy fight.

Many of the bandits much preferred hiding, believing an ambush to be reckless and unnecessary. Luca argued that there were too many to keep hiding. The knights were likely to track them to the meadow, spoiling their chances at collecting the ransom. Luca's men eventually chose to trust him.

In contrast, Sarna held her bow and arrow aimed at the trail but had already decided she would shoot harmlessly at the ground. The idea of her participation was absurd.

At the first glimmer of sunlight sparkling off a sentinel knight's helmet, Luca let his arrow fly. Sarna knew he'd been aiming for the unprotected neck area, but he missed. The arrow bounced off the knight's chest instead. A subsequent volley of arrows did not perform any better. The knights were dismounted with swords drawn in less time than Sarna thought possible. When the bandits sprang from the bushes, two of them fell straight away, their heads wobbling on the ground away from their bodies.

The spectacle of a massive sword fight was far less acrobatic and skillful than Sarna had always imagined. She'd always believed battle to be a massive dance floor of swordplay opponents, but there was none of that. It was a gruesome mess. Rather than striking each other's swords, they struck each other.

The trail became littered and darkened with blood and organs, limbs and heads. Within minutes, the knights' advantage in armor, health, and weaponry took over. An increasing number of bandits lay eviscerated and dying on the ground.

Depleted of arrows, Luca unsheathed his sword and charged from the bushes. With two jabs, he downed two knights, inserting his sword between the joins in their plates, piercing the soft padding inside.

More knights seemed to appear from thin air. Sarna even wondered if this was a reverse ambush. When a blow glanced off Luca's shoulder, he tripped and fell against the heels of a different knight. The knight swung his sword down at him, but Luca was too close. The knight rotated to get a better angle just as another stepped up to help finish Luca off. Seeing him exposed and helpless, three knights standing over him, Sarna stepped into the open.

"Stop!" she yelled, but no one noticed her, only once she began to glow. The light from her grew so bright that most of the combatants were blinded, and they shielded their eyes. One of the knights above Luca remained oblivious and brought his sword down with both hands, meaning to cut Luca in half. Sarna yelled again in protest, and a bluish-white light filled the entire area, killing most.

CHIEF ARLYN

The chief and the rest of the Cathyrnee made camp and waited until twilight. By his estimation, it took a day and a half for someone to make it by horse from the Tartarian castle to the Narlaan Plains. Give or take a couple of hours.

Arlyn paced through the encampment. He felt the chill of the coming night. Despite the cold, he ordered that no fires be built. He wanted them to remain hidden. He felt nervous anyway, exposed by the flatlands and lack of trees.

Two moons hung in the darkening sky, both waning, Sar the larger and Jijig the smaller. The pull of both bodies on each other caused the smaller moon to pulse with volcanic activity, while the larger appeared glossy and smooth, tinged with lavender. The presence of these two moons prevented any form of civilization from being built near the coast. The larger tides of the Ayal Sea made the shore far too hostile to make a home in.

Both moons made for mesmerizing fixtures in the heavens anyway. Arlyn could never stop admiring them, no matter the circumstances.

Gish, his lead warrior, stood at hand. He wore a sleeveless, collarless garment, his plaited hair folded behind his ears. He used a metal file to sharpen his sword, applying even strokes over the blade at a slanted angle. Gish pivoted towards the horizon, and that's when Arlyn spotted it, too—a distant rider galloping towards them. At first, Arlyn's hopes rose, then he realized this couldn't be the prince. Not riding alone. Arlyn and Gish were soon joined by five other warriors who gathered to await the rider's arrival.

Once close enough, he could see the rider was Shuudan, a union devoted to relaying communications between tribes and kingdoms. They rode famously fast and were always heavily armed. The messenger slowed his horse to a stop. He reined the animal sideways.

"I have a message for Chief Arlyn," he said.

"That's me," Arlyn said. "How did you find us?"

"Saw you from the hills. You're hard to miss."

"Where is Prince Shayan?"

"It's in the message." The rider reached into an opening cut within his leather saddle. He produced a scroll from there and handed it to Arlyn.

Arlyn took the scroll and read it. Prince Shayan apologized, but he couldn't attend their meeting. There was a sudden family matter so urgent that it exceeded all other priorities. He would be in contact at a future time. That was the entirety of the message, followed by the kingdom's official seal—a small drawing depicting King Khilji dressed in coronation robes, seated with a scowl while holding a scepter.

Arlyn passed the scroll to Gish, who read it next. Two of the other warriors looked over Gish's shoulder, though Arlyn doubted they owned any idea how to read.

"I don't understand," Gish said. "What are we supposed to do?"

"We're on our own." Arlyn snatched the scroll back from him and ripped it in two. He took a few steps away and halted. "How could I be so stupid? Of course, they're washing their hands of us. All that family has ever cared about is themselves."

Gish appeared confused. "Perhaps the prince is telling the truth? Something unforeseen has happened."

"No, it's because they don't care. We're garbage to them." Arlyn threw the shredded message in the direction of the Shuudan Rider, but the breeze sent the papers fluttering back at his own feet. He stomped back towards their encampment.

"*Ha'wiih*, where are you going, Chief?" Gish called after him.

"To hell with it." Arlyn could feel their eyes on his back, but he kept walking. "Looks like our only hope lies in witches and wizards after all."

8

FHAMTEM

The volcano creature pushed as hard as she could, but her baby wouldn't come. She was Chotgor, a volcano-dwelling race recognizable by their hairless humanoid bodies. Their legs and waists shone black before changing ice-blue mid-abdomen, then ashen-white over their upper bodies. This was the evolutionary effect of having lived their entire lives among atmospheric gases.

The creature's name was Ghatora. She hollered in pain. The baby had become stuck. Her mate Fhamtem knelt beside her in their hut. Her womb emitted an orange glow, which pulsed. After more shrieking and pushing, the baby appeared to squirm loose. Once Fhamtem held his daughter, her moist body went limp. She was dead—their sixth stillborn.

The Chotgor were formed from the volcanoes of the

Oroo Mountains, spawned by the spontaneous presence of the Sünsü during the Great Awakening. The sorcery, combined with volcanic geothermal activity, had transformed thriving communities of thermophilic microorganisms into a race of bipedal beings overnight.

The Chotgor fed themselves primarily from shrubs, ferns, and moss, which grew around the volcanoes, their seeds protected during eruptions or deposited later by wind and birds. However, with no rain, these resources were running low. Added with the frequency of infant deaths, more ritual sacrifices became necessary.

That same evening, Fhamtem, a tribal leader, arranged such a ritual. The epidemic of stillborn births and drought had alerted the leaders to the gods' displeasure with them. None of them understood what they could have possibly done wrong. The gods were unpredictable and vengeful that way.

The entire Chotgor population congregated at their highest temple, centered around a stone slab. The sacrifice would be a male virgin, chosen by lottery. While a circle of drummers pounded thunderous rhythms, the Chotgor boy lay across the stone slab before being tied down. A cloaked priest used a jagged, flint dagger to rip open his body, tearing down through his diaphragm. The young male gave a quick scream and went silent. The priest reached in and extracted his pumping, bloody heart. He placed the organ into a bowl held by a statue of their most powerful volcano god. Afterward, the virgin's lifeless body was untied, lifted, and tossed down the temple stairs. His corpse flopped side over side until landing on a terrace at the temple's base.

Fhamtem choked back the sickening sensation he felt in his chest. Watching the discarded boy rolling like a knotted rag was heart-wrenching. If this didn't please the gods, then what would? Daily life had deteriorated from stable survival to starvation and stillborns. They needed any help they could get.

Fhamtem ignored the commotion. He assumed it had been sparked by the sight of such a young male being sacrificed. Though everyone understood the importance, it was still never easy to witness. The chatter kept getting louder, though. He looked up and spotted the source—a dark-cloaked man standing on a ledge that overlooked the sacrificial platform.

The man flipped back his hood to reveal a square-jawed face framed by long, black hair. Flaring red smoke smoldered from his eye sockets. A stunned hush came over the Chotgor until the wind made the only noise, an anabatic force whistling between them.

"I am here to see Fhamtem," the robed man said.

Everyone stared, transfixed and speechless. Normally, the heat of their lands was far too intense for humans, but here was one who didn't seem the least bit affected. He also spoke their language perfectly. Perhaps this wasn't a man.

Fhamtem stepped forward. He stood next to the

priest. "I am Fhamtem," he said. "Are you enemy or friend?"

"Friend! I am called Seelskan. Have you heard of me?"

"I have not. What do you want?"

"I am sorry for the loss of your child."

A murmur went through the crowd. This confused Fhamtem until it struck him that there was no way the human could have known about his child dying.

"I've come to help you, Fhamtem," the warlock said. "I'm here to help all of you."

"We don't need your help. The gods give us their help."

Seelskan folded his hands. "Your people are dying. You were born from the Sünsü, gifted to these lands all those years ago. And now that incantation is fading. Your family lines are dying out."

"And you are here with a solution for us? How are you able to even be here? Humans can't withstand this much heat."

"I am not human. Not anymore. I am a Dark Shulam. And we are gathering forces to our cause. We're recruiting nations, including the tribal nation of the Cathyrnee."

"How do you understand our language?"

Seelskan kept his smile. "To survive, you need resources, Fhamtem. Raw materials. Oil and metal. *Industry*." As he spoke, he gave his attention to the Chotgor as a whole, as though trying to make eye contact with as many as he could. "You're also dying off because the humans of Jyn are restricting your expansion. Stay living in these volcanoes, and these volcanoes will eventually end you. This environment wasn't meant to support life of your size. You're an anomaly."

Their priest found his voice, his hands still oozing with syrupy, aortal blood: "What are you suggesting?" he asked the warlock. "Should we invade and kill people who have never harmed us?"

"Your race needs unity and strong leadership. Not gods. And certainly not sacrifices. Your society is a failed system, Fhamtem."

"You mock me?" The Chotgor tribal leader picked up the dagger from where the priest had dropped it. He pointed the weapon at the warlock. "You seek to influence me through ridicule? You would even mock the gods?"

"Is this better?" Seelskan held his hand out. A flowering fireball flared from his palm. The flames licked between his fingers without burning them. Every Chotgor gasped, except for those in the back who couldn't see. "There is only one god," the warlock told all who could hear. "His name is Baal. And he is coming."

CHIEF ARLYN

Chief Arlyn, Chieftess Yarlaa, Gish, and three other warriors followed Corsika. They reached a large, jutting rock at the base of the Oroo Mountains. Atop the rock stood a robed figure in shadow. Once close enough, Arlyn was taken aback to see the figure was a young girl, her face stripped with ceremonial markings, small symbols trailing in lines down her cheeks, the bridge of her nose, and across her forehead. Her hair and lips were black. The irises of her eyes shone red, though Arlyn felt sure he was just imagining this. No one told him as much, but he assumed this young girl was a Dark Shulam. She looked no older than fifteen.

The Ghe-Sui and the young girl met eyes and bowed to one another. They remained bowing for a long time.

"Are you speaking with each other telepathically?" Arlyn asked after their bowing seemed like it might go on forever.

Yarlaa shushed him and punched his arm.

His voice did seem to break their trance. Both female shamans raised their heads.

"No, no, no," Corsika said to the young girl, "that's not what we want."

"What's wrong?" Arlyn asked her. He checked everyone else. Gish and the three warriors stood together, wide-eyed with worry. Yarlaa, too. There was something profoundly unsettling about this young girl with her black hair and odd tattoos.

"We shouldn't have come here," the Ghe-sui said. "I should've known better." Corsika turned from the Dark Shulam as if she meant to run away but stopped herself. She pointed at the young girl. "She doesn't know what she's doing. The Dark Shulam are a terrible idea. Everything about them."

The Dark Shulam giggled, the fluttering sound of which curled around Arlyn's lower vertebrae, and he nearly yelled at her to stop it. He looked at Yarlaa, who appeared as unsettled as everyone, if not more so. Gish and the warriors placed their hands on their sword handles, prepared to unsheathe them at the slightest escalation.

When Arlyn wheeled back around, he nearly jumped from his boots. Somehow, the Dark Shulam had moved from the elevated rock and was standing before him. He felt mesmerized. Those eyes. They were indeed red. How had she moved so fast?

"Do I make you nervous, Chief Arlyn?" she asked him, but her voice didn't match her face. Sounded too old. Also, her voice echoed, with a second, deeper voice just beneath.

"You make me pretty nervous, yeah," he told her. "What's wrong with you?"

"Nothing, Chief. Why would you ask?"

"You're scaring our shaman somehow. What did you say to her?"

The Dark Shulam smiled. "Your original king and his royal family were killed by the yelkin some months ago, correct?"

Chief Arlyn nodded.

"As chief, you were then appointed to lead the Cathyrnee," she added. "You've done this task well."

"You know a lot for a little girl."

"The Shulam age backward. I am actually quite old."

Yarlaa spoke up: "Can you help us or not?"

"Your people are being erased from this world," the girl said. "For centuries, the Cathyrnee ruled these lands until religious separatism, the Great Awakening, and a Great War brought the kingdom to its knees. I offer you nothing less than your complete rescue. A return to your rule as the richest, most dominant kingdom of Jyn. But you must do exactly as I request."

The Ghe-sui took a few steps forward, then retreated once more. "Don't listen to her. We should leave. Now!"

The Dark Shulam held her hands out, and her smile dissipated. "Fractured ideologies are destroying these lands. We simply wish to see them reunited under one ruler. King Arlyn. As it should be."

"In exchange for what?" Arlyn asked.

The girl shrugged. "Nothing. Just be better. Treat everyone equally."

"She's lying," Corsika said. She went back to her spot behind Gish. "They'll destroy you."

"We will do no such thing!" the young girl shouted.

Arlyn retreated a few steps himself. Her aura seemed to require more room than he was giving it. "If you're so helpful," he asked her, "why do you look like that? You're disturbing."

"I beg your forgiveness if my appearance is unfavorable. This is just how I look. I only ask that you go easy on your judgment of me since my only sin thus far is looking different from you."

"Am I to suppose you intend the best for us?"

"We split from the Ghe-sui because we grew exasperated with their passivity. Anyone can look around at our world now to see what that's brought us. We only wish to help you. To reunite the nations under one banner, as before. When there was peace."

Yarlaa touched Arlyn's shoulder, meant to reassure him. She said to the girl, "I meant, how would you help us *exactly*?"

"By calling on the powers of the one who understands your plight more than anyone. A mighty spirit capable of bringing everlasting peace. The way it should be."

"I'm leaving," Corsika said again. She walked back in the direction of the encampment.

One of the warriors made a move as if to either follow or retrieve her, but Gish held a hand out, signaling him to do neither.

"Yes, let her go," Arlyn said. He turned back to the young girl. "Tell me why she's so frightened of you."

"She's Ghe-sui. They hate change. Without massive confusion and division, what good are they to anyone? Under their watch, Jyn has experienced nothing but greed and bloodshed. We've also watched a Great War bring death, injury, sexual violence, malnutrition, illness, disability, and insanity. We've watched women and children being killed. Baal will save us from all of that. He will save you from yourselves."

"Who?"

"Baal is a powerful and wise spirit. Baal will rid these lands of the Ghe-sui. And other frauds like them."

"He's, what, a wizard?"

The young girl shut her eyes. She seemed saddened. "King Montrose is a hedonistic, opportunistic bully. King Khilji is a tyrannical warmonger. Their Queens are nothing more than vain, ineffectual attention-hounds. They're sewage, yet they control everyone's lives. You know what I say is true."

"We do have no other choice," Yarlaa said low to Arlyn. "Another yelkin attack like the other night..." She trailed off.

Arlyn rubbed his chin. He looked to Gish. "What do you think?"

His second-in-command responded by releasing his hand from his sword. "I feel like this is fighting evil with just more evil. We're being impatient. I think we should wait for Prince Shayan's counsel."

Arlyn barked a short laugh. "His *counsel*? Where is it? No, I'm tired of being at the mercy of that cruel and arrogant family. No more waiting."

"Prince Shayan is a good man. The rest are worthless, but he's at least reasonable."

"She seeks to summon the spirit, Baal!" Corsika had yet again returned to the group, unable to peel herself away, apparently. "He's the personification of evil. The Fiend. He represents temptation, sin, and death.

Nothing else! Baal is a wicked spirit who will help you to become ruler, Chief Arlyn, but only if you rule *under* him. The gods banished Baal to the underworld—"

"Where he has become a leader and a symbol to the poor and the powerless," the Dark Shulam interrupted.

Corsika slapped her hips in frustration. She bellowed, her voice frantic, "The name 'Baal' even means 'Murderer!'"

The young girl rolled her eyes and gave an incredulous titter. "His name means 'Bringer of Life and Light.'" She then said to Arlyn and his group, "Don't listen to her. She's terrified of the Ghe-sui losing relevance. If they could truly help you, wouldn't they have done so already? They care for nothing but their own influence."

"The Magshaa is the wisest of all beings—"

The young girl spun on Corsika, cutting her off again. "The Magshaa is an elderly trickster who keeps the true power of the Sünsü secret because he doesn't even trust his own disciples with it."

Arlyn accidentally met eyes with Corsika and locked on them. He mutely pleaded with those eyes to dispute the young girl in black. Instead, the Ghe-sui resumed her earlier retreat, except now with tears of helplessness flooding her eyes. Her sobs somehow became more audible the further away she walked.

Chief Arlyn asked the young girl, "How do we start? Return our rule to us. Do it."

THE MAGSHAA

Every morning contained its routine. He opened his eyes and, without fail, thought of how fortunate he was to still be alive. Life was precious, and he owned no intention of wasting it. Despite his advanced age, he used every ounce of his energy and power to develop himself, to extend himself to others, to help in achieving enlightenment for all beings. He always thought kindly of others, never getting angry or thinking badly of anyone. Benefiting the world was his entire reason for existing.

The Magshaa was the most mystically powerful man in all of Jyn. He was believed to be over two hundred years old, his soul seeking a new body each time the one he occupied expired. It was the duty of senior monastic disciples to discover his new body, based on spiritual signs and visions. This was followed by the final determination—a candidate standing under the Magshaa Bells at the entrance of the Ghe-sui Temple. If the bells rang on their own, their new Magshaa was chosen.

He rose before the sun, even when traveling. After his morning breakfast and bath, His Holiness undertook prayers, meditations, and prostrations until it was time for his morning walk around the grounds of the Ghe-sui Temple, no matter the weather.

The remainder of the morning was devoted to studying various Ghe-sui texts written by previous Magshaas. Mid-day brought a vegetarian lunch. To purify his body, His Holiness never ate dinner. Should the need arise, he held discussions with his staff or conducted audiences and interviews. The Magshaa next spent the entire afternoon in the temple, located in the southernmost corner of Burnya, nestled at the intersection of the Ikhar and Mogoi Rivers. They used these rivers to keep their community thriving. Evening meant more prayers and meditation with His Holiness retiring to bed shortly before midnight.

Today, however, this routine was altered. Instead of an afternoon filled with counsel or prayers, the Magshaa had summoned every member of the Ghe-sui to his temple, an event rarely called for. A sea of shamans sat before the front steps of the temple, built and enclosed with wickers. Poles and branches stuck to the roof while multi-colored flags and silken lists flapped from a strong eastern gust.

The Magshaa walked to the edge of the top step, which formed a circular pulpit. Above him hung the Bells, referred to by many outsiders and non-believers as "The Atrocity Bells" since they coronated each new Magshaa. The phrase gained traction until even the Ghe-sui adopted the title, a symbolic fellowship of defiance.

Whatever the bells were called, the unseen forces moving them were a mystery, many claiming they could only be moved by Tigiril the Sky God himself.

"Blessed day to you all," the Magshaa said to the shamans before him. He did his best to project, but the dry air made this difficult. His voice cracked. He cleared his throat and tried again. "I've called everyone here because it appears each of us has had the same nightmare. A whispering child. Three drakksuks flying above an army of shadows. Burning horses. I understand many of you can still hear their screaming, as can I. Can still hear that strange language. I know you wish to understand this dream." He took a moment to wipe his mouth and swallow. It was hot, and he thirsted for a drink of water. "As I'm sure you could imagine, the meaning behind this dream is not good. Could not be worse, I'm afraid."

Grumbling percolated through the shamans. There were numerous exchanged looks.

The Magshaa resumed, "This dream we've shared means we must, as a group, come to a decision on our future, and we don't have long."

This created more conversation, louder this time.

His Holiness held a hand up for silence.

"As the dreams have alerted me, the spirit is named Baal. He has other names. None of which I will speak here. I'm sure you know them."

Several shamans popped onto their feet. Others shouted, alarmed.

The Magshaa held his hand up for silence again, but the gesture was met with even more clamor. He tried to be heard and was drowned out. "We can stand and fight!" He waited for their chatter to dissolve, which it normally did when he yelled. "Or we can flee for the Kholm Mountains," he said. "Find somewhere else to have our temple. Somewhere far away. As for myself, I will stay and protect this temple. I will die if I have to. I will also warn both kingdoms. We owe them that much."

This brought another prolonged uproar. A male shaman called out, faceless from the crowd of so many: "How will this being attack us?"

"I wish I knew, my love," the Magshaa said. "I do know he will find our weaknesses. Each of us. Whatever they may be. He will use our vulnerabilities to tear his way through us."

"Is there any hope for us to defeat him?" called another shaman.

The Magshaa paused. He tried to decide on the gentlest way to break it to them, but there wasn't one. "No, defeating him will be impossible."

The consternation and panic became deafening.

"We must flee!" a shaman shouted.

"Let him have these lands!" yelled another. "No one wants us here anyway!"

The Magshaa could feel their fear and anger building. Though he certainly hadn't expected his flock to react favorably to his news, there was far more panic in them than he might've expected. He understood this was created, not only by news of this apocalyptic threat, but also by being marginalized and exploited by the Three Kingdoms for so long. The Ghe-sui's exasperation had grown long before this day came.

Soon, the Magshaa could hear every voice inside his head simultaneously. He became dizzy. His train of thought abandoned him. Too much to process. He pressed his eyes shut and felt his balance tip sideways. He would've fallen to his knees but was saved by Momaset, his top aide. His Holiness hadn't even known anyone was behind him. The Magshaa opened his eyes, shielded them. The mob went hushed at the sight of their leader exhibiting such weakness. "I'm all right," he said. "I'm fine. Just…I'm hot. I need water."

He heard movement behind him. He took comfort in knowing the sound was the rustling of Momaset racing to fetch him water.

Near the front, a younger but bald shaman raised his hand, as though this were a class. The Magshaa pointed at him. He tried to recall his name, and he couldn't. Even his memory failed him anymore.

"How did this happen?" the young shaman asked. "What brings him here?"

"Chief Arlyn and Chieftess Yarlaa of the Cathyrnee will summon him here. It's happening as we speak. The Chief is desperate to protect his people. The Dark Shulam are helping them now." The Magshaa accepted a mug of water from his returning aide. He downed half the mug before speaking again. "The Dark Shulam have been attempting to summon this spirit for ages. Seems they've figured a way to finally make him interested." He finished the rest of the water, letting it drip over his chin. He licked his lips and looked out at the questioning, fretful faces of his great flock. "We once believed that the Great War was the war to end all wars. It seems it has merely set the stage for the real war to come. And now the question is…what do we intend to do about it?"

The Ghe-sui shamans detonated once more, either arguing with each other or shouting more questions for the Magshaa. The volume was more than he could handle. He withdrew into the temple, helped by two disciples with Momaset leading the way. Though His Holiness was aware of how much another display of frailty had likely damaged the Ghe-sui morale, he still needed to lie down. He could focus on nothing else. He needed rest, then a meditation on how to best handle this. The mere approach of such a spirit had sapped his strength. The Magshaa was lowered onto his bed, and his world went black.

CHIEF ARLYN

The chief and his chieftess revisited the same rock where they'd first met the Dark Shulam that morning. Yarlaa carried a small wooden box that contained the items they'd been told to bring: a small graphite sketch of her and the chief, dirt from a grave, the bones from a black cow, and a dozen yarrow flowers.

The Dark Shulam took the box from her. She knelt while holding the box above her head.

Arlyn took Yarlaa's hand and held it tight. He looked back at Gish and the other three warriors, different ones from last time since they'd refused to come back. Arlyn wanted to make sure the warriors who did come were still there.

"Baal, minii üniin sanald ööriigöö oruulna uu!" the black-robed girl chanted, still speaking in that eerie, double-voiced drone, her red eyes glistening. Her chanting continued for so long that Arlyn suspected the entire event was a ridiculous waste of time.

A small cone of flames materialized at the girl's feet. The flames became a large fire, and everyone stepped back. Arlyn swiveled to Yarlaa to ask his wife if she was still sure about doing this. She grabbed his shoulder and said his name. She told Arlyn to look. The flames had metamorphosed into the shape of a man.

"Is this him?" Arlyn asked the Dark Shulam. "Can

I talk to him?"

The young girl kept her eyes shut. Her lips moved, still chanting but no longer audible.

Arlyn saw the burning man turn his head to him. Yarlaa clutched harder to the chief's arm, muttering, scared witless. Though the man burned, the air became freezing.

Their horses whinnied and raised their front hooves, severely spooked. Their necks yanked at their reins. The warriors went to work at redirecting the horse's nervous energy and perhaps, to an extent, their own. They did their best to trot the horses in a circle. Distract their panic.

"Are you Baal?" Arlyn asked the burning man. "Why don't you talk to me?"

An infinitely forked flash of blue lightning struck just over their heads, followed by a deafening crash of thunder, hammering the ground. Everyone jumped, even the Dark Shulam. *Joppa,* Arlyn thought, *what in Tigiril's Shadow have we gotten ourselves into?*

Chief Arlyn fell into a trance and was given a vision. He saw himself meeting Yarlaa for the first time, so many years ago, making bashful eyes with her as she tutored him. She'd been his mentor at a summer camp for young warriors. They'd fallen deeply in love within hours. Now here she stood beside him, visibly trembling, horrified. He watched his wife's face rapidly change from dancing shadows cast by the burning man's glow.

The Dark Shulam set the box down and motioned

for them to come forward. Arlyn took a step, but Yarlaa resisted. She shook her head. She didn't want to go. The Dark Shulam went to them instead. She told them to hold their arms out, which they did. The young girl tied their arms together with a silk scarf, miming for them to open their hands. After complying, without warning, she sliced Arlyn's palm with a small knife. Before Yarlaa could protest, her own palm was sliced as well. She cried out and tried to move away, but the Dark Shulam grabbed her wrist and forced their wounded hands together. A thread of bright blood seeped onto the ground.

The Dark Shulam began to sing: *"Manus in manu datum est circulus, juncto cum praesens, futura, praeterita…"*

The man-shaped flames sparked, then dissolved until only a sliver of dark ash remained. The ash blew away with the wind, and, like that, the burning man was gone.

"What happened?" Arlyn asked. He looked at the young girl, who seemed confused herself. "Where did he go?"

"I do not know."

"You did something wrong?"

With the burning man vanished, the horses calmed, though snorting still, nervous but no longer wanting to flee.

The Dark Shulam closed her eyes and seemed to pray.

"You did it wrong," Arlyn told her.

She ignored him.

The chief worked at untying his wrist from his wife's. "Where is he?" he asked the young girl. "You nearly cut our hands off, and he leaves? Bring him back!"

"Shut up! I'm trying."

Once free, Arlyn motioned for one of the warriors to bring him a cloth for their wounded hands. The padding of his palm pulsed with an acute agony. Even the most incremental flexing of his hand was excruciating. Judging from the pinched look on Yarlaa's face, her own hand didn't feel much better.

"Was that even real?" Arlyn asked the young girl. "Or was that your boyfriend? Helping you pull off this prank."

She spun on him. "I did nothing wrong!"

Yarlaa winced as Gish wrapped a cloth around her bleeding hand. "You are not helping," she said to the chief. "Be happy that thing is gone. It's for the best."

The warriors were back to standing at attention, hands on sword handles.

The Dark Shulam coughed hard. She touched her throat as she attempted to clear it, but this only brought more coughing. This escalated until she bent over.

"Are you all right?" Arlyn asked her.

The young girl straightened herself and nodded. She doubled over and vomited what appeared to be blood. Yarlaa screamed. The warriors unsheathed their swords. The Dark Shulam collapsed onto her knees and retched violently. She vomited more. The blood flowing from her mouth grew clumpy and heavy, even thudding when it hit the ground.

"Chief, I believe we should get the hell out of here," Gish said.

Yarlaa pulled on Arlyn. "Yes, let's go," she said. "Something horrible is happening."

The Dark Shulam gagged as she lowered onto her elbows, still unable to stop throwing up. She fell onto her side and convulsed. Everyone stood watching her, unable to look away, but feeling they should've started running already.

An object struggled to come out of the poor girl's mouth, its outline visible against her cheeks. Once the object became visible, Yarlaa fainted.

10

KING MONTROSE

The king sat in his robe with Artemis. They were in a private study that Montrose had designated for the Gold Master following his appointment to the position. Montrose had a difficult time focusing since he'd slept so little, having spent the entire evening ruminating over the various consequences of future actions—becoming a polyamorous family, possibly. He was a monarch profoundly concerned at all times with his popularity, always fearing a revolt. It had happened in Burnya before, many decades ago. It was how his own family had come into power.

"Are you all right, My Lord?" Artemis was asking him.

Montrose took a sip of tea, groaning from the drowsiness in his joints. "I hope so. Am I here for you to tell me otherwise?"

"My only wish is to see this kingdom thrive, My Lord. Forever. I want the happy times to never end."

The king sat back in his chair. He gestured with annoyance at the stack of papers on Artemis' desk. "Show me. How are we going broke?"

"As I mentioned before, it's excessive spending. We have no balanced budget law, so taxes, deficits, debt, inflation, all of it is volatile."

Montrose nodded sagely, his chin balanced by two fingers. "What?"

"Between the Queen's charities and you eliminating so many taxes and lavishing so much money on the arts and these elaborate events, we have far more money going out than coming in. It's that simple."

Artemis fell silent, and Montrose noticed him, from the corner of his left eye, searching his face for any response to what he'd told him. The king instead thought of Ozyan, the glossy smoothness of her thighs, the shallow divots along her slim brown torso.

"My Lord? Are you listening?"

"Yes, yes. So fix it. Or tell me what to do, and I'll do it."

"We'll need to raise taxes without hurting our economy. Without lowering the value of our currency. It's going to be a delicate ordeal."

"Maybe we could start taxing these tribes that live on our land? We can tax the Ghe-sui."

Artemis was shaking his head before the king could

even finish speaking. "Those tribes have been there for generations, My Lord, keeping to themselves. To tax them, we would have to first explain to them what money is. It would be a disaster."

"What about the Ghe-sui? They certainly know what money is."

"Off-limits, My Lord. Too many people would fight you on it. They're holy people, and they're only here on our land because they followed our ancestors and supported them in their secession from Cathyrnee."

"We need spending reform," the king said, because he'd heard the phrase somewhere once. *I could kill the Queen*, he thought. *Make it look like an accident. If I had to. Perhaps this wasn't as hard as it sounded.*

"Increase trade with Tartaria," said Artemis. "Increase our growth rate. I understand you and the elders prefer independence in everything, but trade gives us a broader market, My Lord. It can create jobs. Raise wages. Right now, you and the Queen are so popular because you've kept us from war, and no one is hungry. Yet. But give the people more jobs and more money, and your popularity will soar into the heavens. You'll be remembered forever."

"You're telling me to do business with that insane, arrogant tyrant in Tartaria, though."

"I don't savor it either. But who else is there? The Cathyrnee are all but completely destroyed. They've been reduced to wandering the plains like nomads."

I could poison her, the king thought. He needed an accomplice, though. He also needed the poison. Root from an aconite plant would do it.

"Arrange a meeting with King Khilji," Artemis was saying. "Open trade with Tartaria. I would even go with you."

"Anything else?"

"How do you mean?"

King Montrose barked at the door: "Guards!"

A guard opened the door and stepped in, followed by his partner. Both wore a complete suit of armor, consisting of a helmet, mail shirt, and breastplate. They held spears.

"Take this man away and have him killed," said the king.

Artemis chuckled, not believing what he'd just heard. He implored for his life as he was dragged away.

King Montrose snapped back to reality. Artemis was still asking him something, still seated at the table. "My Lord, are you understanding what I'm explaining to you?"

"Yes, yes," said the king. "The economy."

ULAAN

After seeing the impossibly long line of shamans outside the temple, each seeking individual counsel with the Magshaa, Ulaan decided to spend some time wandering the village first. She visited several shops and cafes and did her best not to sulk. One might have thought that for someone like herself, who had brought so much money to the temple from her counsels with Queen Saraal, that she wouldn't have to wait in line to see His Holiness. However, she recognized this as her ego talking and drove the thought from her mind. No shaman was better than any other.

During her walk, Ulaan noticed how, for a man who described himself as "just a simple shaman," the Magshaa certainly lived in a heavily guarded compound. Though His Holiness held daily public teachings at his temple, even if he were absent, his presence would still be felt throughout this place. Framed paintings and sketches of the Magshaa hung everywhere. Every shop contained a shrine to him. Street vendors sold assortments of regalia featuring his face, from prayer beads to incense holders. For better or worse, he had become a commodity. (No wonder his fainting spell had caused so much panic!)

Exhausted from the heat and the crowds, Ulaan sought refuge inside the temple's cultural museum, filled with statues, artifacts, and books. She next visited the Ghe-sui Monastery, which brought back many memories for her, a few still painful.

Ulaan went to the temple to check on the line again. It hadn't shortened much, but she chose to join it regardless. Along the path to the temple entrance, like signposts for the line's progress, stood banners with proverbs by the Magshaa. There was: "Where ignorance is our leader, there is no chance for peace." Also: "The way to change minds is never with anger, only love." Next: "Not getting what you want can be the best luck you could ever hope for." There were others, but the heat took her mind off reading them.

Three hours later, she sat on a pillow before the Magshaa. He looked gaunter and more fatigued than she'd ever seen him. He asked her, without a hint of impatience, what he could do for her. Despite having waited so long to see him, she nearly felt guilty for doing so.

"It's Queen Saraal," Ulaan said. "She's visiting me more and more."

"And this troubles you?"

Ulaan nodded. "She's taking more than I can give. I can feel myself…Well, look at me. Don't I look a lot older?"

"You appear beautiful, my love. And Queen Saraal is a woman of extreme importance. She has done much to help pay for what we see around us."

"But she comes to me now sometimes twice per week. I am using the Sünsü so much that I'm hardly left with the energy to do much else."

The Magshaa looked off, taking this in. "She must be a deeply troubled woman."

"She worries King Montrose will get rid of her if she doesn't produce an heir soon. Also, the king has a pregnant mistress."

"Carrying his child?" the Magshaa asked. He shook his head. "Never mind. Of course, it's his child. And now the Queen feels threatened and wants an answer for everything. She's draining your life energy away.

I see it now. Forgive me. I am very tired."

"What am I going to do, Magshaa? She keeps leaning on me to help make things right for her, but the burden is more than I can manage sometimes."

The Magshaa pinched his nose and squeezed his eyes shut. "I love each of you, but you…my disciples, you keep asking me questions, and I keep giving counsel as though my speech today didn't happen. My love, what I said is real. This threat is real." He opened his eyes, woeful. "The demands of the Queen, or any royal figure, or any living being for that matter, are now irrelevant, my love. I can only repeat what I said in my speech today: Decide for yourself. I understand that what I've just told everyone about the dream is difficult to take in, but everyone still must do it. Our world is about to change drastically."

"Your Holiness, so tell me what to do. Tell me, and I will do it. Anything."

"I cannot. Not this time, my love. You're the one who must decide for yourself. Stay and fight with me or seek refuge with the others in the Kholm Mountains."

"What do I do about the Queen, though? I'm so confused."

"You will do nothing. I will visit Tartaria myself since they have the larger army and will probably take more convincing. I will send emissaries to Burnya and pray we have time."

"They won't believe them. No one will."

"Likely not, my love."

"I feel helpless. I can't just abandon my farm."

"So don't."

"What if I see the Queen before then? Should I warn her? What if she wants my powers again?"

The Magshaa lifted himself from his chair and went to her. He bent and placed a hand to the side of her face. "Ulaan, my love, I have a strong sense you will have a huge part to play in the fate of this realm. I hope you choose to stay, but—as I've said—the decision is yours. In the end."

She felt irradiated from inside. This was all she'd ever wanted to hear from her beloved leader. That she was important. That she was needed. That she endured so much misery for a purpose.

The Magshaa kissed her forehead. "Go ahead and cry. It's all right, Ulaan."

She found his permission for this puzzling, then collapsed into spasms of sobbing. She let it out, unembarrassed, crying harder than she had since learning her husband had been killed. She couldn't stop. The Magshaa kept his hand on her shoulder, and it felt good just to have someone touch her. His hand was so warm.

11

CHIEF ARLYN

He lay next to Yarlaa back in their hut. She had been running a high fever ever since returning. Since that time, he kept her covered with fur blankets, which she alternately wanted smothering her, then nowhere near her. Netting hung over the bed as an extra precaution. Arlyn kept expecting his wife to vomit blood as the Dark Shulam had. Thankfully, his wife had been spared this fate, so far anyway. He felt convinced she was simply traumatized and ill from what she'd witnessed. Arlyn felt a bit disoriented and afflicted himself from it. And also guilty for not burying the poor girl, but they had been so frantic to flee. Seeing a loaf-sized maggot twitch its way out of her mouth was enough to transform the bravest warrior into jelly.

The chief gripped his bandaged hand from where the Dark Shulam had sliced him. The pain was agonizing.

A warrior charged through their hut's leather flap. He held a wooden stave torch. "We must get you both to safety!"

"What now?"

"Yelkin! It's at the southern edge of the camp."

"'It?' There's only one?" Arlyn rose from the bed and gathered his shield and longsword. He'd adopted the habit of wearing his armor while sleeping.

"Only one so far," the warrior told him.

Yarlaa awoke. She blinked from the light of the guard's torch. She held a hand up, her face glossy with sweat. "Are we—we're being attacked?"

"Not yet," the warrior said.

Arlyn stood by the bed. He clutched his sword but felt confused. "Not yet? What is it doing?"

"I haven't seen it myself, but we can't risk you going near it."

"I'm going near it. Lead me." He tightened his grip on his sword's handle. He winced again from the cut in his hand.

A second warrior came rushing into the hut. He seemed perplexed to discover there was a discussion and not panic.

"Is it still there?" the first asked him.

The second warrior looked back and forth between everyone. He nodded.

Chief Arlyn brushed by them. Both warriors stepped out of the hut after him. As they walked with brisk strides through the encampment, Arlyn saw there were already men and boys stirring, snatching up their weapons. He and his new guards gradually formed a convoy as they continued toward the southern edge of the camp. When Arlyn noticed this, he couldn't help but feel empowered, rejuvenated. For some reason, these people still fell in line behind him, still believed in him, even after everything they had been through.

The Cathyrnee reached the border of their encampment, and there indeed stood a lone yelkin. The horned, misshapen giant rocked slowly from one foot to the other, as if readying itself for a charge. The warriors went into a defensive formation, shields up, swords drawn. Upon laying its eyes on Arlyn, the yelkin gave its back to him and wandered off, seemingly to leave. It spun and walked back to where it had just been standing.

Arlyn stepped out from the rest of his men. There were shouts of alarm when Arlyn stepped out even further.

"What do you want from us, creature?" he asked the yelkin.

At the sound of his voice, the yelkin stomped forward, which caused the warriors to move forward as well, coming even to where Arlyn stood. The creature snorted and backed off without taking its eyes from the chief. It retreated towards the mountains.

Arlyn held still and waited for the yelkin to reverse direction again, as did every warrior. Nevertheless, the giant kept going until it disappeared over a hill. The Cathyrnee still waited, not relaxing for a moment. Too good to be true.

"Get ready!" Chief Arlyn called.

Every warrior stood with their feet apart, their weight balanced, upper bodies lowered slightly, prepared to either advance or retreat, depending on what came at them.

Nothing did.

The two moons suspended nearly full in the night sky, gray from their glow. Both satellites gazed down on them as an enormous pair of surprised eyes. A cool wind moved through the tall grass of the Narlaan Plains, swaying it around like fur.

Not one warrior eased their position until they saw Arlyn do so. He stood, lowered his sword, and then everyone did.

"What was that about?" asked a voice on his right. It was Gish.

"Put the lookouts back. Tell them, 'Good job.' Alert me if any of these things come back."

"As you wish."

"That was strange, no?"

"Maybe it was lost. Or the rest are rejecting this one, and it doesn't know where to go."

"Does that happen?"

Arlyn walked back toward his hut, moving through his people. He held his head high and could only pray this event meant what he thought—that their wicked agreement had actually been fulfilled. They were protected. For the time being anyway. He could focus on getting Yarlaa healthy, praying her illness wasn't connected to the devilry they'd witnessed, though he already knew somehow it was.

Chief Arlyn marched back to his hut as did his other warriors, returning safely to their loved ones.

LUCA

Overnight, the bandits sat and lay about in a bleeding, moaning heap. Luca wasn't even sure where they were anymore. His head swimming with post-explosion stupor, he struggled to his feet and lurched off to urinate against a tree. He rejoined the rest. He went around checking on the injured. One man held a hand against his stomach to keep his guts inside. Another held a flap of facial skin from peeling down since a sword had made a shallow cleave in his temple. Predictably, most suffered from cut or stab wounds. For slings and bandages, they used strips of fabric they'd taken from the knights' Tartarian banners.

The last two bandits Luca checked on had died. He went back to his original spot and crashed down. As with the rest of the unhurt, he felt utterly astounded at what he had witnessed, not only because his crew was reduced by more than half, but they had been saved by a form of lethal witchcraft bursting from the princess. This was an event wholly unexpected. One moment, Luca was on the ground, his men dying around him, then a bright flash, and every knight lay dead, most clutching their chest as though their hearts had instantaneously failed them.

Luca spotted his old friend Reshaw leaning against a tree on the far side of the clearing. He'd missed him on his rounds somehow. Reshaw's clothing and makeshift armor were swathed in blood, though it was unclear how much was his own. Reshaw stared, transfixed by Sarna on the other side of the clearing.

Sarna sat apart from everyone, even her friend. The bow and arrow he'd given her were nowhere to be seen. She appeared both morose and frightened, confused as everyone else, if not more so.

Luca chose to greet the friend first. He and Reshaw were companions since sword training for the Great War. They had bonded over their shared disdain for the "arts of fighting." For them, this was admitting they couldn't win a fight with their own natural strength. True soldiers were never masters-at-arms. They were brawlers and born killers. Otherwise, you were a worthless, wealthy, fancy man able to afford the leisure of such mastery. Luca and Reshaw came from farms, both the youngest of two brothers.

Reshaw smirked at his friend's approach. He attempted to neaten his appearance somewhat.

"You hurt?" Luca asked him. "You're holding your arm."

He shrugged, almost imperceptibly. "I might live."

"Can I have a look?" He made a move to examine Reshaw's right arm, but he shielded the arm by moving it towards the tree.

"I'm all right," Reshaw said.

Lucas hesitated, relaxed. "Very well."

He looked over at Sarna, noticing movement. The princess went to her friend and shared something from her hands with her, something which they both ate, a handful of nuts and grains, probably. He was amazed that Sarna could eat in the presence of so much gore and death, perhaps a sign she was adapting to this new, rugged way of life.

"She's a witch," Reshaw said to him, also watching the princess.

When Luca looked around, he saw that most men were watching her, those who could lift their heads. "This is no ordinary princess, apparently," he said.

"We'll have to kill her."

"And why's that?"

"Because she'll kill us!"

"Then what has she been waiting for?"

Reshaw winced from moving, readjusted his hidden arm again. "Have you asked her?"

"She says she has no idea what happened. She saw us getting massacred and cried out for it to stop. And it did."

"Don't let her fry us. Can you do that much?"

While Reshaw spoke, Luca pretended to be busy with his sleeves. He knew his growing affection for the princess would cause jealousy, but he didn't know how else to get the men to behave themselves. For them, there was no reason not to take her and accept the ransom anyway. They already robbed, kidnapped, beat, and killed as a way of life, so why would this be the line? Still, Luca knew that to become too much like them would risk his crew becoming a disorganized gang of barbarians. Lead too softly, and he might lose their respect.

"If she could harm us," Luca explained, "we would've been dead two days ago. We proceed with meeting the prince. Exactly where we said to. Nothing changes."

Another of the bandits walked over to them. Luca recognized him as Insho, one of the taller and more physically imposing members of his crew. His face and neck were a terrain of welts and scar lines. The corner of his mouth had even pinned closed from healed-over skin, which somehow did not affect his speech.

"Smart move," he told Luca. "Needlessly attack a knight patrol and hope some of your men get killed off, so your share of the ransom is bigger."

"That was not needless. They would've tracked us right up to the meadow."

"Hardly matters anymore, does it?" Insho nodded at Sarna. "She's a demon. I say we kill her, then when we meet up with her brother tomorrow, we kill him, too. Take the money anyway."

"We're sticking to the plan. No one is to touch her."

"Are you truly that dimwitted? You still think the prince intends to give us our ransom? That patrol was looking for us!"

Luca drew his sword. "I don't like being questioned. Or insulted. You're making me angry."

Insho drew his own weapon, a shortsword. Reshaw stood between the two men. He used a hand on either chest to keep them apart. Luca gazed down and saw the reason for his friend favoring his arm earlier. Judging from the blood spots on his hand bandage, Reshaw had lost two fingers and part of another.

Luca noticed the rest of the crew watching this confrontation with a sort of stunned weariness. He scanned the area for Sarna but didn't see her anymore. She was gone. He was about to get worked up but spotted her sitting against a different tree, her expensive blue tunic muddied and ripped, her sandals caked with clay. Both she and her maiden were no longer recognizable as nobility of any kind. Sarna's face even still held the camouflage stripes he had painted there. She seemed to be off in her own world.

Insho leaned in and pushed Luca's shoulder. "Hey, shithead—"

Luca slashed his sword with an upswing, but Insho stepped back and used his sword to block. Insho kicked Luca in the abdomen and sent him sprawling back. Luca found his balance, though, and dove forward. His shoulder connected with Insho's waist, but he was too large—Luca found himself hugging him. Before Insho could bring his sword down, Luca pivoted out of the way and went to the ground. Insho's sword came down on air, leaving his entire side exposed.

Luca swung at his opponent's ribs, but Insho was faster than he looked. He swung his sword to block again, then thrust his own sword wildly, a mistake. This allowed Luca to duck and take a step towards him, getting inside his reach. He swung his sword upwards, the blade slicing clean through the taller man's shoulder. Insho's entire arm lopped off and smacked the ground. Before he could even cry out, Luca brought his sword back the other way. It slid easily through Insho's neck, and his head somersaulted free.

Reshaw took out his sword, which Luca hadn't expected.

He took a few steps back into a more side-on stance to reduce his body's target size. He watched Reshaw grinding his teeth, ready to go through with this.

Luca held his ground and kept calm. "You want to come, too? Do it."

"You didn't have to chop his fucking head off!"

"We're still going to do what I say. And I say we travel on to meet the prince. Otherwise, we'll be hunted the rest of our lives."

"We'll be hunted the rest of our lives anyway."

"Right, so we're going to need money."

Reshaw lowered his sword.

"Anyone else here have a problem with me?" Luca saw a few of the men glancing at each other, uncertain. He saw they were frightened. This entire ordeal had spiraled beyond them. When fellow soldiers dropped in droves during battle, it was fairly devastating for morale. Without his display of dominance, Luca knew this could've easily become every man for himself.

Living in the woods like animals these months had caused them tremendous stress. Violence was the only language they understood anymore.

Luca snuck glances at Sarna as he spoke, "If anyone even looks like they're thinking about possibly harming a single hair on the princess' head, they will answer to me! Is that understood?"

He had hoped these words would reassure Sarna, but the expression on her face showed him she was more terrified than ever. He felt curious as to the source of her fright, then remembered he had just beheaded a man in front of her.

12

SEELSKAN

After much walking and some climbing, made difficult by having to carry a lit torch, the warlock Seelskan found the cave he'd been looking for. He entered while holding his torch forward, making sure the cave was empty. It wasn't particularly deep, likely formed by a reaction between groundwater and limestone bedrock. Of all the times he'd ever come here, he'd only found the cave occupied once by a mountain lion. The animal was young and, after much hissing, darted around him and fled.

Seelskan set the torch on the ground and took off his robe. He sat naked near the cave's opening and crossed his legs. His lack of clothing allowed for a stronger interconnectedness to the spirit world. After a bout of heavy meditation, his body floated slightly above the cave floor.

The warlock called forth the spirit Baal as he and other Dark Shulams had attempted countless times, but without success. The cooperation of a defeated and oppressed people to erase the sloth and greed of the other kingdoms would hopefully be enough to finally gain the spirit's interest. This evening, as always, Seelskan received no response. Deciding to try the other, less safe method, he lowered to the cave floor. He reached into his shoulder sack, removed a small fabric mat, and unrolled it. He set an array of animal bones in a row. He used a flinty rock to draw two pentagrams on the cave floor, one for him and the other to summon and bind the spirit.

He knelt in the center of his pentagram and shut his eyes. He followed the sensation of his breath entering and leaving his body. He made notice of when his mind wandered, always returning attention to his respiration. Made sure not to obsess over the content of his thoughts, simply pulling back, over and over again.

"*Attenrobendum eos,*" he chanted. "*Ad consiendrum, ad ligandum eos, pariter et solvendum, et ad congregantum eos coram me!*"

Seelskan sensed he was no longer alone in the cave. He opened his eyes. Standing at the cave's entrance stood a large, black wolf, likely attracted by the noise. The warlock calculated the logistics of diving for the dagger inside his shoulder sack. The wolf was close, too close. By the time he got his hands on the weapon, the wolf would likely be on him already. Seelskan went over in his mind what spells he might use when the animal spoke his name. Its voice sounded inside the warlock's skull, right behind his eyeballs. The wolf walked forward and sat inside the other pentagram. The voice said, "Thank you for inviting me here, Seelskan."

"Your presence honors me." He flinched at how puny his own voice sounded in comparison. "I am overjoyed at your arrival. I shall do as you request."

"Oh, but I've been here. Your sister summoned me. I regret that the force of my entry into this world has caused her death."

He flinched at this news, expected as it was. "She knew it might kill her. She did it anyway."

"Her sacrifice will not be forgotten. I'm sorry I can't offer you more comfort than that."

Seelskan hesitated, caught askance by the demon's politeness. "I had hoped you were here," he said, "but I wasn't sure. No one heard from you."

"I'm getting things aligned, dear Seelskan. And I'm conjuring monsters. Big ones. You won't believe your eyes to see them."

"I've attained the allegiance of the Chotgor. And the Cathyrnee, who are depleted but skilled warriors. Their chief is the one who seeks your aid. I've tried to control the yelkin into fighting for us, but it isn't easy. There's not enough intelligence in them to organize. I'm afraid they would merely see everyone as food and attack indiscriminately."

"You underestimate them. Leave the yelkin to me."

"What of the Magshaa and his followers? The Ghe-sui can be very strong."

In a blink, the wolf changed into a creature Seelskan had never seen before. It possessed a stumpy, pink body with tentacles for legs and arms, and three identical human heads suspended above transparent tubing. "Leave them to me as well," the heads said in unison. "Amass the largest army you can and let me know when it's done. We will march on Tartaria. Slaughter all who stand in your way. We will wipe these filthy lands clean, Seelskan. Start a new civilization free from tyranny and monarchs."

Seelskan trembled while praying and hoped the spirit somehow didn't notice this and mistake it for fear or doubt. It was excitement and awe. After all their work and waiting, they had attracted Baal. He was actually here. Seelskan had always considered himself one of the more powerful warlocks, but this was a presence with a potency far beyond what the warlock could ever possess. His waist felt damp, and he wasn't sure if this was from sweat or if he'd pissed himself.

"It will be done," he said.

The spirit's form changed into an exceptionally large lizard with a black, scaly body and golden, glowing eyes. They lit up the walls of the cave, now covered in hieroglyphics. Seelskan had never noticed them before. A sulfuric stench permeated the cave.

"The Ghe-sui are ignorant and helpless," the lizard

said inside the warlock's brain. "Their abilities largely remain a mystery to themselves. The Magshaa is old and nearing the expiration of his current form. With the wickedness of the royals extinguished, these lands will prosper like never before. There will finally be peace. It's a wonderful thing your sister did by bringing me here, Seelskan."

"I am awash in your greatness."

"I will give you everything. For her sacrifice. You will be the greatest ruler Jyn has ever known."

"I want to be the ruler this world needs."

"I do not doubt it."

"Only one question: You mentioned monsters. What kind of monsters?"

A hot wind blew into the cave and peppered the warlock's face and body with fine sand. He covered his face with his arms and turned away. He gasped and wiped his eyes. He looked back to see that the spirit Baal had vanished.

ULAAN

She headed home, a four-hour trip by horse. Normally, when undertaking such a journey, she would have paid a few of her ranch hands to accompany her. The way to the temple was beset with bandits and predators lately. She had left the farm in such a hurry, though. Ulaan was now forced to brave the night alone. Fortunately, both moons being nearly full kept her way lit, and she was able to keep an eye on her surroundings, especially when stopping twice to feed the horse and give it a rest.

She passed through a couple of villages, but no one came out to invite her in, which was unusual, even for the time of night. She passed an inn, but it was too loud inside, the patrons too drunk. She rode her horse onward and made it back to the farm just before sundown. Once home, she made some tea and stood in her front doorway. She watched the descending sun scatter its colors over shelves of flat clouds, changing the sky from gray to violet. The scenery was so peaceful and gorgeous that it made the idea of an impending evil feel completely far-fetched. Was it possible the nightmare the Ghe-sui had shared meant something else entirely, and His Holiness was in error?

Ulaan dismissed this idea and set about feeding the chickens some leftover fruit peels. Many ranch hands still remained, working quickly to beat the dying light. They had divided into smaller harvesting teams to pick and sort lettuce, radishes, and garlic. When she saw what appeared to be Queen Saraal's caravan cresting a hill to the west, Ulaan's first instinct was to dash back into the cottage. Wash and make herself presentable. Clean the soil from her skin and skirt at least. But she was far too tired. Besides, it was highly unusual for the Queen to visit again so soon. The timing of her arrival meant the Queen had stayed in Burnya for less than a few hours before coming back. Something must have happened.

Noknok raced out to greet the caravan, barking the entire way, then rushing in circles around the squires. They guided the caravan's horses with other foot servants leading the way.

As usual, the stateliness of the Queen's arrival attracted the notice of every remaining ranch hand. They left their chores to watch the caravan pull up. A consort wearing white knee-breeches and a frilled shirt helped Queen Saraal step out of her carriage. Ulaan started to bow but stopped herself.

"I apologize for returning to you again so soon," the Queen said to Ulaan, "but this just couldn't wait."

She took Ulaan by her elbow and led her gently towards her cottage. The Queen's three servants made to follow as normal, but the Queen ordered them to stay outside this time. Noknok sniffed at the Queen's shoes until Ulaan scolded him.

Once inside and seated, the Queen removed her gloves and crossed her arms over her lap. She said, "I want her gone."

A chicken had somehow found its way inside with them. The bird strutted back and forth between the two women as they spoke. Ulaan thought to shoo the chicken outside but was held in place by the Queen's hands on her knees.

"Punished, my Queen?" she asked her.

"I will pay you to place a curse on him. On both of them. A hex. Something to make her go away."

"That's not what the Ghe-sui are about, my Queen.

You would need to find a Dark Shulam for something like that."

"A Dark what? No, I don't want to deal with anyone but you." Queen Saraal's eyes were piercing, pleading. "Ulaan, you must help me. This means everything."

"I will need to speak with the Magshaa first."

"No, no, no, I don't have time for that. I need to get rid of this girl. Yesterday. She's going to ruin my life. And ruin the king's life! She will bring down the entire kingdom."

"I've never performed a curse." Ulaan felt the exhaustion from her long trip inside her bones. Her head hurt.

The Queen leaned in and took Ulaan's hands in hers. "Ulaan, I consider you my friend. I do. I wouldn't say this unless I meant it, but I believe you can do this. You're so strong."

Ulaan wasn't sure how to even begin processing such a statement from the Queen, so she blurted, "Our land has many greater problems that you don't even know about yet, Your Highness. The Magshaa is sending emissaries to Burnya as we speak to warn the king."

"Please, I don't want to involve anyone else," she said, not even registering what Ulaan had said. "Make this wretched slut go away. Some servants confided in me that they overheard her pressuring the king to get rid of me."

"For me to place a curse on someone…at a time like

this. It would be extremely dangerous."

"I'm not asking you to *kill* them. I'm only asking you to help me. Help me save my throne!"

Ulaan opened her mouth to speak but couldn't find words. She didn't want to lose this important connection for her fellow shamans. For her leader. What had the Magshaa said? She should start making her own decisions. She decided if their world truly was under attack from a great and terrible spirit, they were going to need the Queen's financing more than ever, particularly if fleeing Jyn became necessary.

"I know you can do it," Queen Saraal whispered. "Ulaan, please…"

"What do you want me to do? What kind of curse?"

"Make her sick. Make her hair fall out. Make her ugly, so the king no longer wants her."

"I-I can try…I guess…"

Queen Saraal did an incredible thing next. She knelt before Ulaan, who couldn't withstand the sight of this. She hadn't swept the floor yet. A stupid chicken scratched at the floor nearby. She bent down with the Queen. "I will do the best I can, but I've never done a curse before. The Ghe-sui don't do curses."

Ulaan understood harnessing such dark energy could be harmful, take more years off her life than she had surrendered already. Could possibly make her sick. This even had the potential to change her appearance in such a way that other shamans would know what she'd done.

The Queen squeezed her hands harder and smiled.

"Name your price. Whatever it is. Does that help?"

"It's not about the money, Your Highness."

Her Highness gave a small laugh. "Nonsense, dear Ulaan. It's always about the money. Name your price."

As if in agreement, the chicken made a hiccup noise and pranced towards the kitchen.

SARNA

The babsulisk nectar was passed around to help the wounded bandits cope with their pain. After the third bottle was opened, a psychological seal seemed to burst. Sarna could sense that the trauma of battle, even for those unharmed, was proving a formidable adversary to their rest and focus. The intoxicating juice was shared by everyone. The bandits soon banished any awareness of what was scheduled for tomorrow morning, choosing instead to just keep drinking, even Luca.

Sarna sat watching them from outside the campfire light, hoping to remain unnoticed. Beside her, Lalya slept on the ground, perhaps tipsy herself from the few sips of babsulisk offered her. The nectar had brought some color to her cheeks. At least she was sleeping.

With stiff body language, Luca sang. It was a sad tune Sarna didn't know, but she assumed it must've been a lower-class drinking song. A few of them joined him singing, but, for the most part, Luca's performance remained a solo act. He became increasingly drunk, which spawned more singing. Sarna couldn't help but believe his behavior was caused by the guilt of murdering one of his own men in front of everyone. It bothered him.

Once most of his crew passed out—or died, as she imagined was possible—Luca stumbled over to where she sat. She tensed up, unsure how to manage him in this condition.

Ever since bursting with that murderous light, somehow slaying an entire order of knights, the bandits kept their distance from her. Sarna truly had no idea how she'd done it. She had always assumed that feeling different was a residual effect of being born to royalty. Having special tutors and assistants from such a young age would make anyone feel isolated and strange. However, when she managed to make a dish slide across the table by staring at it too long, she knew she was a bit more different than she'd supposed.

One evening, she'd been seated at the table of some dining room or another. Her father had yelled at her for not eating everything on her plate, shaming her for being too skinny.

She greatly feared her father, the king—a harsh, demeaning man who never smiled. Whenever in his presence, she reflexively cowered. Sarna could even see how frightened her mother was of her husband, despite her mother always reassuring her that he loved her. Her father simply had his own way of showing it. Plus, he had a lot of responsibilities on his mind. He had an entire kingdom to lord over. A war to win. The coldness and cruelty were necessary traits of his position.

Queen Abika would attempt to bring Sarna closer in heart to her father by relating tales of how differently her father had behaved when younger. How romantic he'd been while wooing her. The gifts he'd bought her. The rings. How handsome and brave he'd appeared in his armor. How resolute and important he carried himself. Sarna made up her mind to learn to be more like her father, though it was impossible not to fear him.

Then came that evening, age eight, sitting alone at the dining table, tears spilling over her cheeks. The humiliation burned her face, nerves simmering with anger at herself for letting her father down. She stared at her plate and the barely touched food there, freshly caught river fish with fruit and vegetables overly flavored with caraway, nutmeg, and pepper.

The fish stared back at her with glossy, vacant eyes. She willed the fish to disappear, despising the dumb, helpless way it gazed at nothing. The dish scooted away. Sarna thought harder, and the dish slid another yard down the table. She jumped back with delayed surprise. *Wait, what had just happened?*

She knew of the Great Awakening from her tutoring, though it was met with deep skepticism in their mostly secular kingdom. Adding to the skepticism, many who were supposedly blessed with this new magic had withdrawn from society to study their new abilities more closely before anyone could be hurt by it. She'd never been sure whether to believe in the Sünsü or not. Not until that very moment when she'd moved a dish without touching it.

Throughout that same week, she practiced moving items around her bedroom, deciding to keep her ability a secret, fearful of being shunned or punished for it. When her abilities evaporated over time, she dismissed them as a fleeting phenomenon. Even felt relieved to be normal again. Apart from the occasional soft tingling inside her core, like a surge of energy impatient to escape, she forgot about it entirely, and it went away. Easy as that. Still, she could never shake the feeling of an extra sensitivity and awareness towards her surroundings. A sense of aliveness within her that most people didn't seem to understand.

With this came thoughts of home and the struggle to not feel sorry for herself and cry. She missed her mother, or at least the woman she was before the war. She missed her reassuring smiles, her warm, comforting hugs, seeing her sitting across from her and Shayan as children, telling them made-up stories that kept them spellbound. She missed her mother's ability to help her believe in herself.

"Where are you, Princess?" Luca stood over her, wavering on his feet, eyes half-cocked. "Why are you looking at me like that?"

"You're making me nervous," Sarna told him.

"You have your abilities for a reason. You could be the most powerful person alive if you wanted to be. I'm so sure of it. Aren't *you*?"

"Not even slightly."

"What troubles you?"

"I just killed people. A lot of men who did nothing wrong, except try to save me. And I killed them. Every one of them."

"Because you needed to rescue me."

"Because I'm a monster."

He grinned. "Well, then, monster…" He reached out to touch her hair, and she moved her head away. "Won't you kiss me?" he asked her.

"No," she said. "Please, don't touch me."

"Everyone is asleep. No one will know."

"You're drunk."

"And you are nothing special out here." He gestured at the area around them. "Kiss me."

When she didn't move, he gave her a sloppy grin and took a few steps forward.

"Stop!" she yelled, and it came out louder and more panicked than she intended. Both looked back at the other men sleeping, but none stirred.

"Stop me," he told her. "Use those powers. I want to see you do it."

The campfire snapped and hissed, insects chattering, relentless in their hymnal. She felt deep down inside and tried to summon the same power as before to make an invisible shield. She willed it to happen and did her best to feel it happening. She felt nothing but afraid.

Luca made a lunge for her and grabbed the front of her tunic. He tried ripping it open, but the material held. This allowed Sarna to push off and crawl away. He watched her. He blinked a few times until the anger edged back into his face. He caught her ankles and dragged her back. He lifted Sarna by her hair and forced her onto her feet. She searched inside again for the power to defend herself. Where was it?

He let go of her hair, and the relief of pressure off her scalp felt miraculous.

Sarna waited a few beats. She opened her eyes. She saw Luca walking away as he wiped his face. He was crying.

"Are you all right, my love?" Lalya had apparently awoken during the racket.

"I'm sorry I did that," Luca whimpered. "Sorry."

Sarna felt like an idiot. Here, she thought she could use her empathetic charms to blend in and win these men over. Be the royal diplomat beloved by all citizens. All things to all people. But these men were born of a different species. Different everything. How could she have hoped to find respect and admiration from such men? Why would she even want it?

"That bastard," Lalya muttered. She stroked

Sarna's hair, doing her best to comfort her, fulfilling the role of protector herself for a change. "We're going to get out of this, my love. We're going to be fine. Your brother will rescue us in the morning, and none of this will have ever happened."

A shadow fell over the two girls, and they looked up to see the bandit Reshaw, Luca's good friend. He stood silhouetted by the campfire, a mischievous grin etching its way through his left cheek.

"I'm going to kill both of you," he slurred. "Right now."

He downed the last swish from a bottle he was holding and chucked it at the fire. Sarna didn't know what happened to the bottle after that.

ULAAN

Once Queen Saraal and the ranch hands had departed, Ulaan went and stood in the exact middle of her cottage. Noknok scratched at the door to be let in, but she ignored him. She tried ignoring the chicken, but it kept circling her, which she found distracting. She used her foot to usher the bird outside while keeping Noknok from coming in. This required some light acrobatics, but she succeeded. Ulaan walked to the center of her living area. She regarded the large sack of coins the squire had plopped onto the breakfast table. Without even counting it, she could see it was considerably more than the Queen had ever paid. It was more money than Ulaan had ever laid eyes on.

She tried to determine whether the Magshaa would be pleased or annoyed with her. He certainly wouldn't have approved of her performing a curse. But Queen Saraal was a ruler. Her obedience belonged to her as well. Besides, one curse wouldn't end the world. It was already ending. Chances were the curse wouldn't work anyway. She had never done it before and only knew what to do through gossip she'd heard.

Ulaan shut her eyes. If she wanted to move forward with the curse, she had to carefully consider what she wanted to happen. Set her intention. She also needed to protect herself. Cursing someone could bounce back at her, so she wore a special amulet meant as a shield.

She next made a doll to use as a poppet, representing the king's mistress. She stuffed cotton into a small square of muslin, then wrapped the muslin diagonally around the cotton. She cut a piece of twine and wrapped it around the muslin, making a "neck." She secured it with a knot and used the same procedure to make arms and legs.

It was time for the unsavory part, the part that had garnered the gossip. Lifting the hem of her skirt, Ulaan urinated into a jar. She crammed the poppet inside and twisted the lid on. She lit a candle and dripped wax over the lid to seal it completely. While doing this, she imagined scenarios in which the king's mistress made her furious. Ulaan pictured this girl choking puppies and shaking babies, whatever image allowed her to feel hate towards the person, to infuse the jar with every strand of negative energy she could conjure.

Afterward, she went outside to the toolshed nearest the goat pen. Noknok followed. He barked and whimpered, confused and hurt by her lack of attention.

Ulaan found a shovel inside the shed and used it to dig a small but deep hole. She dropped the jar in and buried it. Noknok sniffed at the mound of dirt covering the hole but abandoned it to follow Ulaan back inside. She halted him at the door. The dog needed bathing.

Before bedtime, she decided to get food ready for the animals, including the dog. She let her body do the work because her mind went elsewhere, wondering how long the curse might take. A day? Weeks? A sun circle? If too much time went by with no results, would the Queen expect her money back? It was always possible that the curse might affect someone close to the mistress instead of the mistress herself.

As the sun fell, she fed Noknok, the chickens, and the goats. She collected some hay in a barrel and rolled it to the stable to feed her horses. Now that the curse was complete, she tried to fill her mind with positive thoughts and appreciation for the life she owned. She thought of how she'd had this particular horse since she was young. How there was something about a little girl and her love of horses. The connection and sweetness of that love were so profound. The soft muzzle of a horse seemed designed by the gods for the kisses of a little girl, their thick manes meant for handholds and hugs. Feeling the warm breath of a horse against her cheek, smelling its musky scent. She adored this. It was positive.

It was also a beautiful night, the landscape lit by the twin moons. She admired the round hills in the distance, making for a scenic backdrop to her humble farm, ripe with growing field crops. The air was crisp and clean. Ulaan felt thankful for that, too.

She spotted Noknok sprinting towards her. He barked aggressively. The barking became growling as he gained on her. She noticed his mouth foaming. The horse appeared to sense the danger, and he galloped to the far end of his stable.

As her dog came closer, she saw Noknok's eyes were rolled white. Foam spilled in strings from his jowls. There was no longer a question of whether Noknok meant to attack her.

The horse whinnied and kicked its front hooves. Ulaan stepped backward and tripped. She landed hard on her elbow. Her dog dove onto her, growling and slobbering, wild with murderous rage. Noknok used his full weight to pin her down while his fanged mouth viciously sought out her throat. She tried to shove him off with her forearm, but this was a mistake. The dog sank its teeth there, chewing, drool oozing over her arm and into her face.

"Noknok, no!" she shouted, but she could see from the empty whites of his eyes that this wasn't Noknok anymore.

Despite the violence and pain, Ulaan steadied her mind, doing her best to conjure the Sünsü and save herself. It was her last chance. Noknok meant to kill her.

"*Shok-chok*!" she yelled, her voice reverberating.

The dog went flying and landed some distance away. He skidded on his paws and yipped a bit. She watched as her dog rapidly recovered and charged again.

Ulaan held both hands up as if braced against an invisible barrier. She braced her left leg out behind her.

"*Shok-chok*!" she shrieked, louder this time, before her dog could make another leap.

A gelatinous blast of blue aural air struck the dog, and he cried out. As soon as the dog landed, Ulaan launched another blast wave, and this caved in the dog's ribs, folding them over until they punctured the skin on either side of his body. Her next blast came out by accident, a hysteria spasm. It crushed Noknok's skull, putting the poor dog out of his misery. His tongue lopped outside his mouth, covered in a mass of frothy blood.

Ulaan ran to her dog and cradled his shattered head in her lap. She wailed loud enough to bring several straggling ranch hands running in from the fields. She was devastated. This dog was like her child. An object of unconditional love, the ultimate companion for security and comfort. Now shredded and taken away from her.

The arriving men recoiled from what they saw, which was Ulaan cradling the mangled corpse of her most beloved pet. The men took their hats off.

14

SARNA

She shielded her friend behind her. Both girls backed up while the large, drunken bandit advanced on them. As Lalya fell, she reached out for either side of Sarna's shoulders and found both, bringing Sarna down with her. Sarna landed on top of her.

"So, Princess, witch, whatever," Reshaw slurred. He fumbled with his sword. "You'll need to be killed first. Somebody should've done this a long time ago."

Sarna managed to find her feet, yank Lalya up with her. Watching as this bandit advanced on her, Sarna recalled some wisdom her brother had once shared: "A man can be tall as any mountain, be the meanest, ugliest heathen alive," Shayan had told her, "but kick him in the crotch hard enough and he'll fold like a paper blind."

Reshaw grinned, pleased by the sight of them so scared. The princess saw her chance. She brought her leg up and connected the instep of her foot solidly against his groin. Both girls yelped as he tottered backward. He grimaced in agony and squashed his eyes shut. When he reopened them, she could see the rage there, the pure primal impulse to punish. He growled and pounced at them.

Sarna grabbed Lalya's hand, and they ran into the forest. Holding hands slowed them down, so they dropped their hands and kept running. The moons lit their way, but Sarna still caught the occasional branch whipping her face. She kept checking back, expecting to see their assailant directly behind them. She spotted Reshaw giving chase, but the pain in his groin kept him from making long strides. His arm and hand also seemed hurt. Sarna pushed Lalya to keep running. *Go, go, go.* The campfire light became completely blocked out by trees, and they were left to navigate by moonlight alone.

Lalya bumped into a tree. She shut a hand over her mouth to keep from yelling. Sarna reached out to find her friend's arm but couldn't. They were in shadow.

"Wait, wait," Sarna said. "I have to rest just a moment." She hobbled out of the shadow and into the moonlight. Her joints were tightening up, and she felt light-headed.

"We don't even know where we're going," Lalya whispered.

Sarna coughed. "We…we need to just…just get

away."

Lalya seemed to notice the princess wincing. She reached out and tucked a shard of Sarna's hair behind her ear. "My love, are you hurt bad?"

"I'm fine. We need to keep going." Sarna looked around, fully realizing how vulnerable they were. Two girls with no weapons in a forest filled with beasts.

Sarna saw Lalya's eyes go wide with surprise and fright. She didn't hear the footsteps until they were right behind her. She ducked, and the bandit grabbed air and tripped over her bent body. Still intoxicated, Luca hit the ground. There was a moment's relief when she saw it was Luca and not the other man. She took off running regardless. She didn't see Lalya anywhere.

Luca recovered and sprang after her. She saw Lalya running to her left, so Sarna went farther to the right to draw him away.

He called her name, pleading with her, but she kept running, branches slapping her face, cutting her cheeks. Twigs and rocks scraped her feet, but nothing stopped her, not even when her hair got snagged by a thorny branch. It broke off and dangled in her hair, bouncing against her neck. She darted from one shadow to the next, the trees above her grating the bright moonlight into a scattershot grid around her.

Luca kept calling to her: "Sarna…Sarna, please! Please, stop…Stop!"

She ran out of breath. Her ribs cramped, and her

joints went rigid. She realized she could never outrun him. She convinced herself she would stop for just a moment, but when she did so, she found she could no longer use her legs. She heard Luca wheezing from somewhere behind her. He had stopped as well.

"I-I'm sorry," he said. "Sarna, I'm so sorry. I-I'm drunk."

She turned to see him doubled over while holding onto a tree. His other hand clutched his side.

"You put your hands on me," she said, her voice low with anger. "Never saw that coming. Not from you."

"I know, I know. I behaved horribly. And I'm sorry. I'll never do it again. Never."

"I don't even believe you."

He straightened. He looked around them. "Where are you even going? You both can't survive out here by yourselves."

"No, we're much safer with you and your friendly colleagues."

"We're going to meet up with your brother tomorrow morning. You'll be freed."

"What's to keep you or your men from killing us the instant you have your money? You would do *anything* to get back at my father."

As he spoke, he came closer to her until he stood right in front of her. "Kill you? Why would I ever do that? That's crazy."

"That *is* crazy. You're crazy."

"I just drank way too much...and I was scared.

When you're the leader, there's always someone trying to knock you off. Look, give me your hand. I'll protect you from here on. You have my word."

"We have to find Lalya. I'm not going back without her."

He reached out to touch the side of her face, but she moved it. "Let's run away," he told her. "Just the two of us. Forget the stupid ransom."

"You truly are drunk, aren't you?"

"Not anymore, no."

"My father and brother would never stop hunting you."

"I don't care, Sarna."

"You've lost your mind."

"I don't even care about the ransom anymore. All I care about is you."

"You've known me for three days, and now you expect me to just disappear into the forest with you? Live out our lives, running from my family forever? Eating squirrels and berries?"

"Yes."

"Not in a million years, Luca. Not if you were the last man in all of Jyn." Sarna checked their surroundings but couldn't see far. There was nowhere she could run. She didn't see Lalya anywhere.

"Marry me," he said. "You can tell your father to forgive me, can't you?"

"I could tell him anything, but he would still have you executed on sight."

"I'll take that chance. I can't even control myself."

"That's the truest thing you've said since I met you."

"Be with me." Luca placed his arm around her. He rested his hand on the small of her back. He guided her gently towards him and kissed her. He hesitated but kissed her again, pressing his body against hers.

"You're a lowlife," she said. "I want nothing to do with you."

He nodded and kissed her again.

She held her hands up against his chest, but he held on. She kept pushing until the warmth of his lips against hers became a distraction, and she went limp in his arms. Sarna wanted to run, but she was too exhausted. This seemed the easiest solution. Tolerate him, just for this moment. She would make him think he'd won her over, but she would run. As soon as she found the strength. She would escape.

She folded her arms around his neck, and her lips opened to accept his. She rested against his strong, sturdy body, felt his hands glide over her back, the soft hairs on her arms rising.

They sank together towards the ground.

KING MONTROSE

He visited Ozyan in her servants' quarters. He had her set up in her own room, many floors away from the rest. Though this made her the target of scorn and jealousy from the other servants, she couldn't have cared less. At least that's what she told him. He grabbed her in his arms and kissed her neck.

He had just visited the Queen's quarters but found her gone again. He searched the entire castle, enquiring with anyone he crossed paths with. A servant girl informed him that the Queen had left in the afternoon, heading back east again. Delighted, he went directly to Ozyan. Always to Ozyan. She matched his kisses, giggling.

"I absolutely have the most wonderful news to tell you!" Her entire body and face beamed.

He guided her towards the bed, still nuzzling her.

They reached the bed, but she resisted falling in. "Wait, My Lord. I'm serious. You're going to be so happy."

He gathered his patience and stepped back. He went to the door and checked the hall for eavesdroppers. He returned. "I am ready to be happy," he said. "Out with it."

She joined her hands beneath her chin and grinned, savoring the moment. She ran in place from the excitement. She stopped running and said, "I am with child."

He let this sink in. "Pregnant?"

"Three months, I think. We're going to have a baby, My Lord." She tilted her head. "Aren't you happy?"

He suppressed a laugh. "I don't know what I am."

"I thought you would be ecstatic. I don't understand."

"Take off your clothes."

She gave him a curious look but did as she was told, letting her robe drop. She shrank from the morning chill in the room. She rubbed her arms and arched her back. She pushed her chest forward and resummoned that confidence he admired so much. He tried to imagine their child growing inside of her, but he couldn't picture it.

"Tell me you're happy?" she asked, unable to hide the utter dejection in her voice.

"You're not the Queen yet. My dove, we'll have to get rid of it."

"'*It?*' What do you mean?"

"Ozyan, you cannot have this child. Not here in the castle anyway."

She clutched her hands over her stomach. "You mean to murder our child?"

"You know about the Queen's miscarriages."

"That's why I thought you would be pleased." A small tear spilled from her left eye. It made a wet line over her cheek before dripping off her chin. "This could be your heir finally. The one you've been waiting for."

"Maybe I'm fine with the way things are."

"All kings need an heir! Also, you said you loved me! You said you would make me your Queen. If this isn't the perfect excuse, there must not be one."

"There isn't." He touched her face. Her eyes leaked rivulets of tears.

She moved out of his grasp and lifted her robe from the floor. She slid her arms through the robe's sleeves while speaking: "You lied to me."

"I never lied to you. I'm doing this *for* you. If the Queen found out you were carrying my child, there's no telling what she would do to you."

"You're the most powerful man in all of Burnya! You can do anything you want!"

"And so can she! That's what you don't understand."

"I always suspected you thought I was stupid! But not *this* stupid!"

"Keep your voice down," he whispered. Montrose snatched her forearm. "I am still your king! You will do as I say, and what I say is that you will tell no one about this child. This child will go away, or else *you* will. Is there anything about that you don't understand?"

She tried taking her arm back, but he held on. "You're hurting me!" she cried.

He let go. He folded his hands over his head to keep from grabbing her again.

Ozyan sat on her bed and hugged herself. "I never expected this. Never. It's like I don't even know you."

King Montrose was made to leave the room and saw a vase of ghost orchids atop a brass flower stand. He shoved the stand to the floor, where it smashed loudly enough that Ozyan yelped and jumped back. She went still, silent, shocked. With the echo of shattering ceramic still in his ears, he charged from the room and slammed her door shut behind him.

15

SHAYAN

He rode his horse at the head of the other knights, also on horseback. The sun had risen a few hours ago, followed by a full day's march. Already the heat was intolerable, made worse by the amount of armor he wore. As a child, Shayan had romanticized the idea of wearing a suit of armor. It exaggerated the features of a knight, making him appear superhuman. Their armor made them gods. Now that Shayan had to actually wear full armor again as part of a quest, he detested it. It was like wearing a man-shaped oven. Making matters worse, he'd chosen to skip the Aimaar Forest and travel the Orgoon Plains because of its openness. This also meant a lack of shade, though.

Knights on either side of him carried tailless, rectangular red flags bearing the Tartarian banner: an eagle with its wings spread, shielding the two moons of Jyn. There was no wind, so the banners swiveled like wet towels atop their spears.

Just before midday, Shayan sent out a small band of knights and mounted serjeants to range ahead and scout the trail for potential threats. He planned to circumvent the Aimaar Forest and meet the bandits in a meadow that bordered the southern edge. Cutting through the forest itself would have saved them a day, but Prince Shayan decided not to risk an ambush. The forest had already taken his sister. Shayan had no intention of being next.

The knights and serjeants rode out to check for any bridges or choke points. Both required advanced protective forces since either left them vulnerable. When Shayan saw his outriders returning, he assumed this was why. The Ikhar River contained a myriad of tributaries on its eastern side, many of them too small to be drawn on a map. Shayan and his knights would come across a bridge sooner or later. They had to.

One of the scouts lifted his helmet visor to speak. "We've come across a caravan of Ghe-sui shamans, accompanied by the Magshaa. They say they are traveling to Tartaria to meet with the king."

"Where did they get that idea?" Shayan asked.

"They say they have a warning for him. A great evil is upon us."

"That's true enough. How much money does he want?"

"He didn't mention money, Your Highness."

"How far away are they?"

"Not far. They're wishing to avoid the Aimaar Forest, same as us. They're just over those hills. They should become visible at any moment."

The prince motioned his men to ride on. As the scout predicted, they soon spotted a long row of robed travelers ahead. They met them on the trail. Shayan watched from his horse as servants lowered the horizontal poles of the Magshaa's palanquin from their shoulders. They set it down while various servants had already helped the Magshaa get out.

Shielding his eyes, the old man approached the prince. Shayan could not believe how old and frail this man appeared. This was the great and mighty Magshaa? Did people give their faith and money to this trembling man? He appeared just barely capable of standing, with wrinkled skin so thin and brittle as to be nearly transparent.

The Magshaa smiled. "Greetings, my prince," he said.

"What do you want with my father?"

"I've come with a dire warning for him, I'm afraid. I wish to have counsel with the king."

"That is absolutely not going to happen."

The others in the Magshaa's caravan looked at each other, dismayed. The Magshaa, for his part, seemed unfazed. "Then may I pass the warning to you instead, Your Highness?"

"As long as it doesn't involve a speech."

"His name is Baal. He is a powerful spirit capable

of killing everyone in this world. He was summoned by the Cathyrnee in a desperate attempt to save themselves. They didn't know what they were doing, but it's been done. He is here."

"Is he? Where? And he's going to kill everyone? What's he waiting for?"

"I don't imagine he's waiting at all, Your Highness. He's simply arranging matters in a way that makes his conquest the easiest."

"My people can handle themselves against any threat. Always have. Thank you for the warning, though. We'll be careful."

"He doesn't intend on leaving any of your people alive. Not a single man, woman, or child. No one. The Ghe-sui either."

"What will he do with an empty world?"

"Leave it to rot, I suppose. He is The Destroyer. Many of my flock are preparing to flee for the Kholm Mountains. Perhaps some of your people would want to go with them."

"Why not stand and fight if it means the death of everyone? What do you have to lose?"

The Magshaa's smile faltered. "The Kholm Mountains are a harsh place. Living there will never be easy."

"And you're hoping it's bad enough that nothing or no one will care to follow them there."

"Exactly, Your Highness. Baal will have the aid of every animal in our realm, no matter how small or monstrous. We have seen it in our dreams."

Prince Shayan chuckled. "How much money do you want?"

"Why would I want money?"

"After your sermons and prophecies, there's usually a fee required."

"I can see you're skeptical of our intentions. You hold us in contempt because of our attitude of neutrality during the Great War."

"Look, old man, just get out of here before we trample over you. You will go nowhere near the king. Ever. Turn around and go home."

The Magshaa bowed. He backed up until he no longer stood on the trail. His caravan followed his lead and cleared a path for the knights to pass.

"Good luck getting the princess back," the Magshaa said.

Prince Shayan made a kissing noise, which was his horse's cue to start slowly. He galloped past the Magshaa and down the corridor of shamans lining the trail. He caught the meaning of what the old man had said to him and halted. He pulled his horse to backstep. "How did you know about that?" he asked the Magshaa.

"I love you, Your Highness," the old man said to him. "I beg you to reconsider your perspective on what I'm telling you."

Prince Shayan glared at the old man, trying to decide what to do about him. A part of him wanted to know how the Magshaa could be aware of the princess' kidnapping. It was impossible unless the old man had played a part in it. He contemplated having the old man arrested but decided against it. Keep the focus on rescuing Sarna. Anyway, he couldn't have word of his father's mental condition spreading.

"Get your witch doctors together and go home," Prince Shayan said. "I'll wait."

The Magshaa bowed in consent. He smiled and nodded at the nearest Ghe-sui who could see him. They walked back up the trail.

A younger, more stern-looking shaman came near, his bald head topped with a black ponytail. He was the only one who dared show offense towards the prince.

"Don't come near me," Shayan told him. His hand went to his sword.

The shaman stopped. "I am Momaset," he said.

"Good for you. Now go. All of you. You people stink."

The Ghe-sui walked with Prince Shayan and his knights as far as the northern perimeter of the Orgoon Plains and split off.

Before doing so, the Magshaa instructed his shamans to give the knights their remaining water. This made Prince Shayan feel somewhat ashamed, but he accepted the water anyway. Riding inside all this iron and metal had reduced his physique to a skeletal shell by now. He was sure of it. He envied the Ghe-sui for their light robes.

"Will you pray for us, old man?" Prince Shayan asked him. "I'm not religious, but some of my men might be."

The Magshaa closed his eyes and held his open palms towards them. He muttered a while, then smiled and nodded at the prince. Shayan wasn't sure what had come over him to make such a request. The morale of his men maybe. They weren't being paid much.

"Sorry that I can't allow you to visit my father," Shayan told the Magshaa. "If you knew the reason, you would understand."

"I do understand," the Magshaa said. Most of his caravan had already changed back towards the southeast from where they had come. Most hung their heads as if marching to their death. Their white robes made them resemble an endless row of pointy teeth, lined beneath an immense blue sky of shaggy pink clouds.

QUEEN ABIKA

She tossed and turned in bed, unable to shake the image of Sarna being mishandled. Of Sarna lost and alone in the forest, controlled by men who rejoiced in her anguish. She also kept seeing her daughter but as a toddler, her face red and dripping with tears. Queen Abika couldn't take it. She repressed the need to cry and slipped into an uneasy sleep. She awoke just after midnight to find the king awake and sitting up beside her. He stared intently at the dormant fireplace against the northern wall, which, apart from some seat furniture and the balustrade around their bed, was the only thing he could stare at. They kept their royal bedroom relatively bare. When she waved her hand over his face to get his attention, King Khilji didn't flinch.

"Mother?" the king asked the fireplace.

The Queen felt confused. Did he mean *her*? He had never called her that, but there was no one else in the room. "Khilji, are you dreaming?" she asked him.

"What are you?" he asked the fireplace. "Are you what I think you are?"

She touched his shoulder and gave it a light shake. "Khilji, who are you talking to, dear?"

"Is that your real name?" The king still addressed the fireplace. "What are you doing here?"

"There's no one there," she told him. She didn't know what to do. She considered getting one of the guards outside, but what more would they do, except witness this odd behavior and report it to every person they came in touch with?

"What do you want from me?" the king yelled.

"Khilji, you must stop this! There is no one there. Who do you think you're talking to?"

"Leave my family out of this!" The king moved to the bedside as if meaning to stand, but he didn't. "Why would you appear to me that way? Get out of here!"

"Calm down, please. You're dreaming." She still didn't want the guards to come in, but he was getting louder. Shushing him wasn't working.

"This world is not done with me!" King Khilji bellowed. "How dare you!"

The apothecaries who had examined the king that day claimed he was merely getting old. His mind was becoming soft as it did with many elderly. They assured the Queen she should not take it personally. The king's mind was simply not well. He was no longer able to control his emotions and had no understanding of how upsetting his behavior was to everyone. The Queen tried to remind herself of this. To not be afraid. Not to blame herself. To treasure the time when he wasn't like this.

Abika had never expected to become a Queen, but once it happened, she dedicated her life to serving Tartaria and supporting her husband in his onerous responsibilities as ruler. At the outbreak of the Great War, some in her court urged her and their children to evacuate to Burnya or the Kholm Forests. She wouldn't hear of it. She would never abandon her husband or her kingdom, and neither would the children. She and her family had endured the dangers of war with every citizen.

Now that the war was over, her challenges had become more personal. Since the king's behavior had turned volatile, Queen Abika and the prince fulfilled most of his public engagements. She was becoming the kingdom's matriarch, whether she cared to or not.

She reached out and touched her husband's shoulder again. "Don't get out of bed."

His attention would not be moved from the fire-place, and whoever he thought he saw there. He lowered his head as though listening to someone. He gave a small, sardonic laugh. "No, I don't think so." For the first time, he seemed aware of the Queen touching his shoulder. He looked at her and narrowed his eyes. "Our daughter has been kidnapped?"

The Queen stopped dead. Who told him? She sat with her mouth open, unable to respond. Did Shayan tell him? Perhaps the king had overheard a conversation somehow?

"Why would you keep something like that from me?" the king asked her. His voice wavered between anger and hurt.

"Who told you?" she whispered.

He pointed at the fireplace. "He did."

"Khilji, my dearest, by the gods, there is no one there!"

"Look harder."

Queen Abika gazed where her husband pointed. She looked harder at the fireplace, even at the masonry wall opposite the fireplace, then back and forth. She saw no one.

"Just leave us alone," the king said to the fireplace. He rose to his feet. "You have no dealings here!"

"Shh! Don't yell," the Queen pleaded. She began wishing the guards would hear and come in already. Take over.

Khilji turned his attention to the window. "Kill myself? Ha!"

Now the king spoke of suicide. The Queen had her reason to go fetch a guard. She got out of bed, threw on a long silk overcoat, and ran for the door. She opened it and saw both guards already facing her, having heard what was happening, but hesitant to enter.

"No!" the king yelled at the window. "You will not touch me!"

Before she could get a word out to either guard, she spun at the sound of the king's footsteps padding across the floor. King Khilji dove at the window, and impossibly, his head went through the glass, slicing his face in crosspatches. It was a stained-glass window made from a combination of sand and wood ash and should not have broken. The king reeled backward while holding his bleeding face.

A reflex of duty, the guards rushed over to help him, which seemed to trigger a response in the king to flee. In two fluid motions, he opened the window and leaped. He tumbled hundreds of meters downwards. She heard him hit—a bag of bones slapping the ground.

16

KING MONTROSE

The King of Burnya returned to his mistress' chambers as if nothing had happened. He made love to Ozyan, then held her. They lay inside his throne room, her right leg thrown over his waist, her right arm wrapped over his enormous stomach, getting larger by the day. His weight gain was even becoming an issue. He suffered backaches, joint pain, heartburn, and hemorrhoids. Stress was catching up to him physically.

He lay still for a time until Ozyan asked him what he was thinking about, surprising him. He believed her to be sleeping.

Montrose rolled onto his side to face her. He placed a hand on her stomach. He traced the tips of his fingers through the shallow valleys bracketing her navel. He thought of their baby inside.

She touched his face. "Why do you look so sad?"

"I wish I had met you first, and I wouldn't have this mess to deal with."

"If it wasn't for the Queen, I wouldn't have been her servant, and we wouldn't have met. How else would a village girl get inside the castle?"

"I might've spotted you at one of my speeches. We could've found each other somehow. We didn't."

"I feel sorry for the Queen. Getting old. Being so lost over her place in the world that she's addicted to fortune tellers. It's pathetic."

"So I'm having you taken back to your village."

Ozyan laughed but realized he wasn't laughing. "You've decided that?"

"I cannot allow you to have this baby right under the Queen's nose."

"But she doesn't know it's yours!"

"There are a thousand people living in this castle, and each of them has eyes. Everyone knows already. Someone will tell her."

"I'll go back to my village and have our baby in secret, then you send for me later?"

"I might send for the child. I haven't decided. If it's a boy, I'll send for him and make him my heir, get the public off our backs about it. If the child is a girl, you can keep her and marry her to whoever pays the highest price."

"So you never want to see me again?"

"Precious sweetness, you're gorgeous, but we met each other too late."

She jerked away from him and sat up. She pressed her back against the headboard. "So that's it? You're getting rid of me?"

King Montrose nodded. He watched the shock wash over her face and posture, and it pleased him. He could do anything he wanted to her, and there would be no consequences. Nothing she could do. The potential for cruelty was exhilarating.

"Yes, I have decided this," he said. Or his mouth did. "I'm sending you away. Don't ever come back."

"How could—? You promised me the throne!"

"That was before you got pregnant."

The king lurched out of bed and went to the door. He called out for his bodyguards. Two came running.

"Take this girl back to her village," he told them. He felt his chest sink. He didn't want this. Why was he doing it? His words came from someone else.

Both guards marched a direct path to where Ozyan lay as if already expecting this to happen. Ozyan cried out as they grabbed her. One held her from behind while the other clutched her ankles and fought to control her thrashing legs. After they left the room, the king listened to her screaming all the way down the hall. He hadn't even told them which village. He had no idea where they were taking her.

King Montrose went back and sat on his bed, his hands shutting his ears. He remained this way even though he could no longer hear Ozyan because she was gone.

CHIEF ARLYN

Arlyn squeezed his wife's hands. He'd been watching her sleep for so long that he couldn't take it anymore. He understood she needed the rest. A mysterious illness had laid siege to her body, and she needed to shut down, focus all her reserves on fighting it. But she kept getting worse. She consistently sweated yet was ice-cold to the touch. She would sometimes open her eyes but wouldn't respond, not even to her name. She needed a medicine man, but they were all dead. The best Chief Arlyn could do was an apprentice who wanted only to treat her with herbs, which he made into tea. Getting her to drink this tea was a laborious task. She could barely keep conscious for it.

Arlyn heard the flap of his hut move. "Is he here?"

"Yes," said Gish.

The chief groaned his way to his feet. "Lead me to him."

He followed his head warrior outside, expecting to make a trek to the encampment's perimeter. But the black-robed figure stood right outside, adjacent enough that Arlyn nearly ran into him. He'd imagined the warlock's eyes would be the same as those of the Dark Shulam girl, but this man's eyes were not just red but glowing, burning. A molten mist smoldered over his brows without singeing them. His needle-straight black hair enclosed a well-formed, strong-jawed face.

Three warriors, a scout, and Gish encircled the man, hands on their sword handles, ready to pounce should the warlock choose aggression for any reason.

"I am Seelskan," the man said.

"You've come to discuss our deal," Arlyn told him.

Seelskan grinned. He lifted back his hood, and a strand of hair fell in his face, covering his left eye. The hair didn't burn. "I have indeed," the warlock said. "The next stage of it anyway."

"I had a meeting with my tribal leaders, and we've decided there is no next stage. No deal. We're out. We don't want any part of what you're planning anymore."

Seelskan frowned. He butterflied those brows and whistled. "This is a distressing development. I'm afraid it's too late."

"We figured you would say that, but we don't care. It was a mistake. You can leave."

"Baal has come to restore the kingdom of Cathyrnee. To return your people to their rule. He's already set events in motion."

"Such as?"

"King Khilji is dead."

"I don't believe it. How?"

"He jumped through the window of his throne room."

"And why would he do that?"

"Because Baal convinced him to."

Arlyn lowered his head, shook it. "Even if that's

true, we still don't want your help. This was a huge mistake. I'm sorry."

Seelskan swept a confused look at the men around him. "I just don't understand this. What other hope do you have?"

"We don't even know, Skelskan—"

"Seelskan."

"—But I can't side with people whose eyes glow red and who wear black all the time. Gives me little faith that we would actually come out ahead with you."

"You're completely wrong!" The warlock shrank after the warriors took out their swords. He'd scared them. He made sure to lower his voice: "What worries you, Chief Arlyn? What changed?"

"Watching that young girl die like that. You weren't there. She died horribly. Then there was a man made out of fire, and he made my wife sick ...somehow." Arlyn shook his head, then grabbed it. That memory. It kept jolting him. "No, thank you. We'll make do on our own."

The warlock laughed, incredulous. "This is nonsense. That girl was my sister, Mya, who knew precisely what was going to happen, but she understood how important this was. She gave her life for you. And your wife is sick because she's dehydrated, malnourished, and living in the open plains like an animal."

"If you're such a powerful wizard, then come heal her."

"I cannot heal your wife."

"Right. What good are you?"

"I don't know that kind of sorcery."

"So I couldn't expect you to heal any of my men should they get hurt?"

Seelskan rolled his head, more frustrated. "I came here tonight to ask you to accompany me in a meeting with the Chotgor. They are willing to join us. All of us together will make a formidable foe against Tartaria."

"You're telling me the Chotgor are real."

"Their leader would meet you at the base of the Oroo Mountains. Perhaps you should meet with him before making your final decision. They are a strong species and ready to fight."

"Then they likely don't need us. Our minds have been made. We will survive on our own. That's the end of it."

Seelskan gave the armed men around him another look. He shouldered his way out of their circle and paced a short distance away. He turned back and bowed. He ran a hand through his black locks. "Let me know if you change your mind. I will come back tomorrow to check."

"There's no need. No!"

Seelskan looked at him, and his glowing eyes appeared to dim. Arlyn noticed just how profoundly grief-stricken and nervous the warlock appeared.

The warlock shook his head. "Baal wants to make this a better world. To clean these lands from the disease of corrupt and wealthy royals who care nothing for the troubles of the common people. Baal would make you the greatest ruler ever, Chief Arlyn."

The warlock made his way through the encampment until disappearing behind a distant row of huts. His entire path was lined with other Cathyrnee pausing in their nightly chores to watch this mysterious, strange-looking man as he passed them.

"You did the right thing," said Gish. "The cost of their help was too expensive."

Arlyn blinked a tear out of his eye. "He's going to keep coming back."

The Cathyrnee Chief gazed up at the two moons. He was aware of his men looking at him worriedly, feeling the same truth: Like it or not, the deal with evil had been made, and there was ultimately nothing they could do to break it. His conversation with Seelskan had meant nothing.

17

SARNA

The princess felt a chill mist against her face. It was a sensation strange enough to make her open her eyes and discover she was floating among the tree-tops. Heart hammering in her chest, she became winded with panic. She peeked between her feet to see the ground some hundred meters below her. She gave her head a hard shake, hoping to wake herself, but instead gulped when she felt her elevation dip. Fearing she was plunging back to the forest floor, she stiffened her body and windmilled her arms until she realized she was no longer falling.

She'd always held a fear of heights, so staying silent was a struggle. She looked around herself for attachments, wondering if she were tied up here somehow, affixed to the trees. Branches and leaves touched her on every part of her body, but she could still see both moons above, near enough to touch. They showed her that nothing held her up. She was indeed floating.

She and Luca had spent the day traveling through the forest, sometimes running, other times walking, stopping only to kiss or hold one another. They knew they were losing ground by doing so, but they couldn't help themselves. Sarna had never felt like this for any man. His broad shoulders, narrow waist, and his V-shaped torso. There was also his height, that masculine facial symmetry. He was a man with goals which he actively pursued, however misguided. His single-focused energy shattered resistance, and she couldn't help but be drawn to it, despite his earlier conduct towards her. She excused his assault as just being part of his way, but he could be changed. She could change him. She knew this because, for better or worse, he was always fully present with her, whether through eye contact, listening, or talking. He was there. Luca saw her as no one else ever had. He knew which berries to eat to keep their energy up! He was smart in a way that mattered more than books.

Besides, being with him was a vast improvement over the sheltered, sanitized existence of the castleliving she had known before. She was here because she wanted to be. It was why her powers had obliterated those knights but were absent against him. Had to be.

Between the branches below, she spotted Luca

sleeping, using his tunic as a pillow. At the sight of him, her body lowered. She shut her eyes and concentrated on an image of herself coming down. Sarna felt her feet contact the ground. She held her arms out for balance until, sure enough, that she could stand on her own. She looked over at Luca. She felt sure she had awoken him. He didn't move, and he'd seemed such a light sleeper, an expected requirement for life on the run. She walked over to him and knelt.

Sarna reached to touch him. She experienced a memory of her father falling, except it wasn't a memory. She recoiled and stood. She saw her father falling again, but the image was stronger. She perceived an impact and nearly lost her footing, already convinced this was tied to why she had levitated.

Did she just have a vision? She thought of the Ghesui leader, the only person in Jyn who had come close enough to mastering the Sünsü, this mysterious magic randomly gifted to their world. This leader was likely the only person who could help her. Something was happening inside her, and she needed to gain control of it before it took control of her. She was having visions now. Most importantly, she had to know if her father was still alive.

What she'd seen changed everything. The world reversed in a millisecond. Her twisted but budding romance with this rough, handsome bandit would have to wait.

She looked at the sky to get her bearings. Both moons slid towards the east, which meant the Ghe-sui Temple lay to her left. She decided the Ghe-sui could help her. It was her only choice. She could make it there by tomorrow night if she departed this instant. She thought of poor Lalya and where she could be. They had searched for her until Luca convinced Sarna they should head out of the forest first. If the other bandits caught up to them, they would kill them both. Sarna argued to keep looking, but Luca had made up his mind.

She gazed once more on his sleeping face, completely at rest, his Y-shaped facial scar glowing in the moonlight. Such a beautiful man, but so wrecked. Her heart broke for him. She would miss him, though she now understood she would've left him behind in the end anyway. His personality was too volatile, and she was too independent. It would never work.

Sarna thought of Lalya again and how to find her. She needed help. They both did.

She tiptoed off into the darkness. After gaining enough distance to be out of earshot, she broke into a sprint.

KING MONTROSE

Back in his private chamber, he awoke at midday. He stared at the ceiling. Normally, he rose much earlier. He would start his day by going to the chapel and praying. Not that he believed in the existence of higher beings, but he knew this ritual was expected of him. A superstitious formality. He would next eat a light breakfast and spend the rest of the day attending meetings on laws that either needed to be passed or repealed. It was hard to keep up. This morning, he just skipped it. All of it.

He'd been unable to sleep the entire night, rolling around in his mind his reasons for having Ozyan returned to her village. Apart from the obvious and the rational, he genuinely couldn't put his finger on why he had done such a thing. Perhaps because this was the easiest solution. She wouldn't stop pressuring him, and he'd simply reacted. There was only so much he could take.

Lunchtime came and went, but he had no appetite, still too distraught. Attendants checked in on him several times, but he kept dismissing them. Told them he didn't feel well, which was true. So lovesick and shocked by his own actions. He considered hunting with his dogs to take his mind off his woes. A few tumbles of thunder brought a hard rain, which extinguished that idea. He heard excited conversations outside the window, too many to be simply caused by the rain.

King Montrose elbowed his way out of bed and went to the window. He saw the outer doors of the castle open to admit the Queen and her convoy. She was arriving with great fanfare, made even shriller by the simultaneous downpour. It was the last thing the king wanted to see. Felt nauseous at the thought of it. He was too upset, too heartbroken right now.

He wanted his quietude. Also, Queen Saraal would see the grief in his face and know why it was there. She would make life worse.

The king dressed and raced for the garden courtyard, a recently renovated feature of the castle, the largest of its kind. Eight hundred acres in the midwest section. Woodland patches had also received an elaborate facelift. It had cost a fortune.

On his way, the king passed two attendants who wordlessly fell in behind him, following him until he found a stone bench to sit on. The bench was wet from the rain, but he didn't care. He noticed the attendants standing there. "Get away from me," he told them, and the attendants obliged.

Montrose removed his shoes and dug his toes into the grass. He felt overcome with the urge to weep. Ozyan was gone. Banished. An act she would never forgive him for. What had he done? For the first time in his life, he wished he weren't king. But he was, and the only way to get his mistress back was to get rid of the Queen, which was impossible.

King Montrose buried his face in his hands. And how to explain to Queen Saraal why one of her servants was missing? He supposed he would think of something. Lies came easily.

"My Lord?"

He turned to see a thin, young man with a bowl haircut, adorned in the burgundy breastplate of a Shuudan Rider. He held a twine-bound scroll towards the king.

"King Khilji is dead," the Rider told him. Montrose noticed the boy trembling. His eyes shone red as if he'd been crying.

Montrose took the scroll and unwrapped the twine. He rolled the scroll open and read it. The message indeed confirmed what the Rider had just told him. The funeral would be held in two days. His presence, as well as that of the Queen's and their highest-ranking nobility, was requested. It was an official letter from Queen Abika.

"Why are you crying?" he asked the Rider. "You liked that piece of shit?"

The Shuudan Rider nodded, sniffled.

"What's your name?"

The boy mumbled something which Montrose couldn't hear. "My father used to work in the castle as a gong farmer," he said. "I got to meet his Highness once when I was younger."

"Your father cleaned the king's toilets, and you admire the king instead of your father?"

"It was still a high honor, My Lord."

"You both must've been quite fond of King Khilji."

"He was nice to me, My Lord. To us. He never had to be."

"How did he die? The letter doesn't say."

"He jumped. Through the window of his throne room."

King Montrose thought this over. "*Joppa*," he murmured.

The Rider looked around the courtyard, as if uncomfortable, uncertain of what more was expected of him, slowly understanding he should've just kept his mouth shut and his emotions under control.

"So he was nice to you once, and that's all a king has to do, I suppose," King Montrose said. He nearly reached out to touch the boy but didn't.

"He wasn't perfect," the Shuudan Rider said. "But he was kind to me. He was always kind to my father. He led our kingdom to victory in the Great War. He kept the war away from our kingdom, which was what he'd promised us."

Montrose sat with this in his mind. "Thank you for bringing this letter to me. I am sorry to hear of your king's untimely death. I am sure, no doubt, there are many, many more good people as despondent as you are."

The boy bowed but remained standing, waiting to be released. Instead, King Montrose ruminated over the image of King Khilji falling to his death, the way his body must have exploded gruesomely from the ground's impact. He suppressed a smile. Or tried to. He smiled anyway. The king's death could be his opportunity to save his kingdom's finances. With King Khilji out of the way, Montrose could find more power over Jyn. More leverage. Prince Shayan would make a worthy king, but far more naïve and easier to manipulate than his father.

Of course, he and the Queen would attend the funeral! It was a two-day trip, weather permitting. Plenty of time for any form of mayhem or danger to befall their procession. They would be vulnerable. The Queen could get killed.

"Do you truly love your father?" King Montrose asked the Rider.

The boy looked at him, perplexed. "Very much, My Lord."

"Would you do anything for him?"

"He would do as much for me. Anyone in my family would."

King Montrose reached out and took one of the Rider's hands in his, pressing his other hand over the top of it. From a branch nearby, a bird sang in abrupt, well-spaced notes, then finished with a trill.

"How would you like to be rich?" the king asked the boy. "Rich enough that you would never have to risk your life to bring another message to anyone. Rich enough that your father would never have to clean anyone's shit ever again. Would you like that? Say yes for me."

18

THE MAGSHAA

It was well into the next afternoon when the Magshaa's rejected caravan drew near the Ghe-sui Temple. Every diplomat, political operative, attendant, and assistant traveled with him in silence. Their spirits, of course, had been dampened by Prince Shayan's careless dismissal of their warning. The Magshaa could only pray that the emissaries sent to warn the royal family of Burnya would be more successful. However, it was already known that King Montrose's view of them was nearly as contentious, due to their influence over Queen Saraal.

Riding in his covered chair, the Magshaa contemplated what he could have done wrong to cause the rest of Jyn to distrust them so much. During the Great

War, he'd decided not to impede on the affairs of warring kingdoms, following the same policy of the kingdom's territory they occupied. He'd underestimated the frustration engendered by those seeking the aid of the Ghe-sui. His inaction was interpreted as impotence, which had now seriously heightened the possibility of a much worse war. He pondered what he could have done differently, but if there was anything, he didn't see it. He stuck by his belief that peace was the way. It would always be the way.

When the rain started, the Magshaa did his best to lighten the hearts of those around him. He signaled for those carrying his palanquin to lower him and help him get out. He walked among those in the caravan and got wet with them. He remained informal, holding their faces as he spoke to them, frequently kissing their heads and chuckling. The mood among the travelers did improve until they were within sight of the temple.

Once they reached the main property, a foul odor wafted towards them. It gained strength. By the time they reached the front gate, many in the caravan doubled over and retched from the overpowering stench. It was the unmistakable smell of rotting flesh. Even the Magshaa was forced to cover his nose and mouth with a scarf.

Crossing the temple grounds, he noticed a complete lack of noise or movement. A few more steps, and the silence was replaced with gasping, then weeping as those in the caravan spread out and saw the large, drying swaths of blood spilled over the stone ground. Horses, monkeys, sheep, dogs, cats, chickens, and llamas lay scattered or in piles, most adjoined by a sickening soup of entrails. Every single farm animal of the Ghe-sui Temple had been slaughtered.

The Magshaa stood befuddled until he was approached by Baeri, the caretaker whose family had served as custodians for the temple, generation after generation. Clothed in a white robe splotched in red, he bowed his head to the Magshaa.

Baeri's cheeks glinted with tears, old and fresh. "I don't know what happened." His voice was strained, barely audible. "They just began attacking each other."

The Magshaa went to remove the scarf from his face but coughed. The smell was too much. It filled the property like a haze. "When did this happen?" he asked.

"After you left. I was cleaning the horse stables, and I heard a racket outside. Your Holiness, you could never imagine the sight. And then the horses—" The caretaker hid his face with his hands and shook from his blubbering.

The Magshaa patted Baeri's arm as he wandered past him. His Holiness took in the sight of so much unrestrained carnage. Flies convened in active clouds over the carcasses.

Other Ghe-sui shamans made their way out of the temple. Seeing their distressed expressions and postures, he understood how truly traumatizing this was for everyone here. The Magshaa closed his eyes, and, for an instant, he endured the single-mindedly murderous impulse of each animal determined to kill the other. It was a sensation so sudden and overwhelming, he swooned. These animals were their friends. To witness them reduced to stinking piles of shredded meat and viscera was the apex of derangement. The Ghe-sui held all life as sacred. The event would've been no worse had they found the shamans themselves in this state.

The Magshaa knew Baal likely had not gained full power yet in their world, but this was his next best effort. It was a warning. He would gain such power here before long. It was in their interest to give up and try to flee. Or so the evil spirit wanted them to believe.

More of the Ghe-sui emerged from the temple. Though pale and trembly, they greeted the caravan with hugs and their own tales of what had transpired.

The Magshaa sensed someone walking beside him and looked to see Momaset, thought of lately as a younger, more virulent version of the Magshaa. Momaset even headed the council, which coronated each new Magshaa in accordance with the ringing of the Magshaa Bells, always perched above the temple entrance.

"This has to do with the dream we all had, doesn't it?" Momaset asked him.

"Yes."

"What should we do?"

"Clean the temple. Round up anyone who has the constitution for it. We will provide every animal with a proper burial."

"As you wish, Your Holiness. But I meant—"

"I know what you meant. This was an attack. It's a display of power."

"He means to scare us into surrendering."

"To damage our will and our minds. For some of these shamans, their own death would've been preferred. He knows that."

"We should all leave."

"As I have said, those who wish to leave, I will not keep them."

"You still wish to stay?"

"Yes."

"I beg you to reconsider, Your Holiness."

"This is where I belong. I cannot leave."

"We can build a new temple. Though we hold this place as sacred, it's all wood and stone in the end. It's not worth dying for."

"Where else would we have gotten the sustenance of two rivers? This land has been good to us. To my people. This temple is my home."

Momaset puffed his cheeks while looking at the ground. At his feet lay a dead monkey, its poor tiny head twisted backward. Momaset blew his breath out. "I respect your will, Your Holiness, and I always have," he said. "But I cannot agree with this."

The Magshaa regarded his pupil. Momaset had

once been as close to him as his own shadow, but recent age had seen him become more independent and questioning of his Master. He understood Momaset's increasing belief that it was time, due to the Magshaa's advanced age and diminishing powers, for Momaset to take charge. This was his chance. His reluctance to abandon the Magshaa came only from a reflexive loyalty.

The Magshaa resumed walking towards the temple, and Momaset joined him.

"All of my power, my studying, my teaching, my meditation," said Momaset, "and now here we stand at the precipice of a great threat—the greatest threat ever—and I don't know what to do. I feel useless."

"So don't be useless. Lead. Gather those who wish to leave and lead them."

"The Ghe-sui must live on."

"I agree. Go."

"Many will refuse to leave you."

"And I welcome any who stay."

"But they will be killed because of you!"

The Magshaa swooned again. Holding his head, he fell to one knee. Shamans standing nearby saw this and rushed over.

"I'm fine, fine. I'm fine." He straightened rapidly as he could, already annoyed at having caused another scene, creating more worry and doubt. At this moment, he caught Momaset standing under the temple entrance. He gazed up at the Magshaa Bells as if anticipating their movement, willing them to ring while he stood under them. Make it official. The Bells remained unmoved.

The Magshaa held his hands up until he had everyone's attention. "My children, remain calm. I know this is difficult to cope with. We need some volunteers to help bury the animals. Meanwhile, let's group the women and children, including the older children, those not old enough to fight, but old enough to protect. Those who wish to stay and fight, we will do our best to repel this evil attack. Otherwise, you can join the women and children or others who wish to leave. Momaset will lead you to somewhere safer, as I've instructed him."

The Magshaa saw and felt the gaze of everyone and fed from it. He tried to give back the energy it had supplied him. Instead, he saw and felt their sadness, and it was crushing.

"We will forgive the entity who did this to our animals," he added. "Forgiveness doesn't mean 'forget.' This action was serious, and it was wrong. Still, the Ghe-sui are not simply in favor of life for the unborn, or the innocent, or for those we care for, or even for those whom we consider good, but for all. All life is sacred because the gods created all life. This is what lies behind my most difficult command to you: Love our enemies and pray for those who persecute us. *Love* them."

A majority of the Ghe-sui bowed to him, still covering their mouth and eyes from the smell. Others looked to Momaset to judge his reaction.

Momaset returned a hard look at them, which soon softened into resignation. "I'll get a shovel," he said. He went inside the temple.

SHAYAN

He rode towards the Thygoras Meadows with a dozen handpicked knights. Their circuitous route cost them another few hours, but they made it in time. Protected by the knights, three pack horses stood, loaded with the ransom coinage held in large side bags. The weight had been enough to require slower travel with frequent water and rest for the horses.

After arriving, Prince Shayan and his knights waited at the northern edge of the clearing, scanning the wood line on the far side of the meadow. No sign of the bandits yet.

To the east, metal-gray thunderclouds rumbled near, filled with lightning. Worried chatter concerning the tardiness of the bandits changed to worry about the oncoming storm.

Shayan saw a light flash across the meadow. Four men wearing sporadically placed armor emerged from the trees. Though their gait appeared unthreatening, the knights drew their longswords. The bandits walked towards them, but they did so slowly while keeping their own weapons tucked away. Shayan saw that Sarna was nowhere to be found among them. He tensed up. What deception was this?

With their tallest member positioned slightly ahead of the others, the bandits halted before the prince and his knights. "Good morning, Your Highness," he said.

"Where is my sister?"

"I am called 'Reshaw,'" said the head bandit, his right hand heavily bandaged. "I fought for your father. My own family was raised—"

"I care nothing about your story." Shayan leaned forward on his saddle. "Where is my sister?"

The bandit winced and averted his eyes. "We have a problem."

An uneasiness spread through the knights, which caused it to spread through the bandits. The horses even stirred.

"A problem," Shayan echoed, then to Reshaw: "Where is my sister?"

"We're going to help you find her, Your Highness. I have the rest of our men already hunting for her."

Shayan noticed the other bandits' eyes darting around. They were nervous. He didn't like this. He took his own sword out and held it at his side. "Where is my sister?"

"We're not sure what happened, but it would seem that our former leader has fallen in love with your dear sister. He and the princess have run away together."

Knowing Sarna's impulsive and roguish nature, he knew how plausible this might actually be. He still wasn't convinced, though. With a measured glare, Shayan met the eyes of each bandit. "I am giving you the count of ten to hand over my sister. After which, we will cut each of you into little pieces."

"Told you he wouldn't believe us," said the most anxious-looking of the bandits. "*I* wouldn't."

Shayan looked them over again and said, "Ten …nine…"

"We didn't have to meet with you," said Reshaw. "We could've fled for the deeper woods, but we wanted to let you know what happened. Let you know it wasn't our fault. We took a chance by appealing to your sense of reason."

"Eight…Seven…"

The bandits' body language told Shayan they were prepared to make a run for it. He didn't care. This was the last thing he needed. His rage became like lava bubbling at the mouth of a volcano.

"I am sorry this happened this way," said the bandit named Reshaw. "This was not our plan."

"Six, five, four…Kill them," Shayan said.

The knights charged. The bandits managed to draw their swords but were overrun instantly. They didn't possess much in the way of armor, so their superior Tartarian steel sliced through them, dismembering each without much effort. The bandits were slain without a single knight suffering a scratch.

"What idiots," one knight muttered while cleaning the gore from his blade.

Shayan took off on his horse. He rode it hard across

the meadow and reached the far wood line. He slowed to a gallop as he traced the meadow's southern edge. He peered into the woods for any sign of Sarna, or more bandits, for anyone. Fat raindrops pinged off his armor. A wrathful thunder reverberated across the darkening sky. Though it approached midday, the storm clouds kept much of the forest in shadow, so he couldn't see much.

Prince Shayan felt a swift and solid impact against his left upper arm. He looked and saw an arrow lodged there, having found purchase between the plates of armor. A masterful shot. Or an extremely lucky one.

He felt no pain, though he could perceive the arrow's tip touching bone. The flesh around the entry point registered the arrow's every movement. A surge of bright blood coated his armor until his entire arm went red. *Who was the idiot now?* The arrow was likely a double-edged broad head, which could've shattered his arm bone were it given slightly more force.

The knights charged over, having seen what happened.

Shayan rode to meet them. He halted to inspect the wound as it finally began hurting, sliced with a thousand tiny razors. As though feeling the prince's pain, his horse tensed his chin, tightened his chewing muscles.

While one of the knights helped him examine the injury, Shayan cursed himself again. His frustration and need for action had caused him to react too hastily. Charging ahead like that had been one of the more foolish things he had ever done. He was fortunate not to have taken more arrows in worse areas of his body. As it was, he was losing blood, albeit slowly.

"Are you all right, Your Highness?" asked a different knight. Shayan was becoming dizzy. "You look pale."

Prince Shayan motioned his good arm at the other side of the meadow. "Go find my sister and don't come back until you fucking do!"

THE MAGSHAA

Harder rain battered the roof of the Ghe-sui temple. The Magshaa sat on a pillow in his private chambers and meditated. It was the best way to solve every problem, focusing on the moment without distractions. Tap into his subconscious mind while becoming as still and calm as possible. Dispel negative energy.

"Your Holiness," a voice said, and the Magshaa knew something was amiss. Not once in a hundred years had anyone ever interrupted him from meditating. Snapping from his trance, he heard and felt the buzz of voices and movement inside and around the temple.

He opened his eyes and saw Momaset there in the

doorway, his face creased with worry. "The time has come," the Magshaa said.

"Yes, people are leaving," Momaset said. "Also, we've received word from a Shuudan Rider that King Khilji is dead."

The Magshaa sat there, disoriented because a Shuudan Rider should never have been necessary. His powers should have alerted him to such a profound event as a king's death. Yet it hadn't. He was stunned.

"How did he die?" he asked.

"The message didn't say."

"It's part of Baal's plan. All will gather to the funeral and be slaughtered at once. He's made it easy for himself."

Momaset started to speak but hesitated. He lowered his head. "Everyone is leaving now."

"I am aware, yes."

His pupil spoke at the floor. "We owe Jyn nothing. For generations, we have served as healers for these people, only to be shunned and blamed for doing what they wanted us to."

"People detest the truth. It is the burden we bear."

"Come with us. Leave. I'm begging you, Your Holiness."

The Magshaa struggled to his feet with Momaset's help. The old man still held onto his pupil's forearm as both entered the temple's main area. They shuffled between floor-to-ceiling shelves holding countless ancient books. A scattering of shamans bent on the floor while praying and chanting over their Ghe-sui prayer books. These were leather-bound journals given to the Ghe-sui at the start of their training, in which they wrote notes and ideas. Pages might also contain drawings and dream interpretations.

"What of the others who live far outside the temple?" Momaset asked.

"They know what's coming. They will make their own decisions just like everyone else."

"This is no death for you, Your Holiness. You deserve a peaceful end."

The Magshaa stopped to touch his pupil's cheek. "You will do fine," he told him. "You are ready."

"Yet I've passed beneath the Bells a thousand times, and they never ring for me."

"Perhaps when you stop counting."

Momaset laughed at this but caught himself.

"No, it's a time to laugh," said the Magshaa. "Go ahead. Laughter is mighty." He continued walking. He stepped between the shamans as he walked the length of the temple. He used both hands to open the doors wide, needing his full strength to do so. A sharp band of golden sunlight impaled the dark clouds, an illumination strong enough to silhouette the long Ghe-sui procession heading out, some on horseback.

Momaset joined him in the doorway, once again glancing up at the Bells there.

The Magshaa smiled at him doing this. He gazed back at the departing shamans. Many caught his eye and looked away, full of shame, but pushed on by their fear. The misery of every one of them settled into the Magshaa's soul. He could see it in their eyes and posture—they felt defeated.

Most left on foot since their horses had been slaughtered. The only horses remaining were those taken on the previous caravan. The only sound was of their feet brushing over small rocks in the trail, leading them away from the temple. This noise combined with the clanging of cooking equipment dangling from shoulder packs. The ground remained muddy from the rain and coated their legs halfway up their calves. Not one of them spoke.

19

CHIEF ARLYN

His newest hut consisted of wooden spokes radiating from a crown, resting on a circular lattice wall, attached with animal hide and ropes. Wooden columns stood in the middle over a brick stove, but the structure was still easily collapsible. Since it had become essential that they stay on the move, the huts were now lightweight enough to be carried by horses and oxen. They could be reassembled in under an hour.

Despite such innovations, the condition of the Cathyrnee worsened. Many of his tribe had abandoned him, fleeing west to Burnya after word spread that King Montrose was accepting refugees. There were also numerous suicides.

Arlyn remained preoccupied with his beloved. He'd remained bedside with her throughout the day, using a piece of felt to wipe the sweat from her face. Her fever simply wouldn't break. She would occasionally open her eyes, and he would try to make her drink babsulisk, as the apprentice had instructed. Sometimes she would, other times she stared at him blankly while the juice overflowed her mouth and drenched her chest. Attendants frequently changed her water bowl.

The flap covering the hut's entrance was yanked aside. It was Gish. "Yelkin! They're coming!"

Arlyn leaped from the bed, still dressed in armor. "How close?"

"Scouts just spotted them. Very close."

Arlyn could feel the ground tremoring. He heard the shouts of his warriors as they prepared for the onslaught.

He followed Gish outside, and the right wall of his hut caved in and was swept away. Legs the size of logs trampled through the encampment. Arlyn and his top warrior brandished their swords, but not in time to prevent two of Yarlaa's attendants from getting scooped up, then bitten in half at the waist. Clothing and flesh hung shredded between the yelkin's fangs. Arlyn spun to see the rest of his hut torn away, carried off on the knees of other giants stomping through.

He moved towards his fallen home, where Yarlaa was buried in a heap of wood. He couldn't even see her. The chief's way became blocked by other warriors fending off more giants. Panicked tribespeople called out while dashing between huts, many holding children. Arlyn heard screams from every direction, even above. He realized some of the noise came from the yelkin themselves, mimicking their prey, creating even more confusion and chaos.

Dogs snapped at the heels of the yelkin, but this had no effect. Many of the dogs were either stamped flat or eaten. Warriors did their best to organize an attack formation. They swung their swords against a passing leg or raised foot, but most were swept aside.

Arlyn shouted at Gish to get the men to retreat to the western edge of the camp. Make a perimeter there. It was their only hope.

The ground shook with enough force from the yelkin's heavy footfalls that it was hard to even stand. Their black eyes burned with hatred. Warriors, women, children, animals, all disappeared beneath their feet. Those who weren't stepped on were picked up and swallowed. It rained blood and bowels.

"Follow me!" Arlyn yelled. "To the perimeter! The perimeter! Make a perimeter!"

Arlyn ran with Gish, not far behind him. At first, it didn't seem as though many warriors obeyed. Another check over his shoulder showed increasingly more warriors running in the same direction.

He needed to advance to a point where they could launch a decisive counterattack against the giants. This would be done by the archers, the captain of whom had noted a weakness in the yelkin's skin around their neck and deltoids. Once enough of the warriors ran together behind Arlyn and Gish, the yelkin noticed and gave chase. With their much longer strides, it took little time for the giants to gain on them. Many warriors in the rear were slapped away, killed by the blunt force exerted against their entire bodies. Chief Arlyn and his remaining warriors kept running.

They reached the edge of the encampment, where Arlyn reversed direction, a signal for the rest to follow. They did their best to duck from the sweeping blows and huge feet, stabbing their swords wherever they could. The resistance this gave was feeble but enough to temporarily prevent the yelkin from advancing.

Arlyn had chosen to set camp in this area of the plains since it lay settled inside several knolls. It was where he had stationed his archers, who now let loose with crisscrossing volleys of arrows. As the arrows found their marks among the yelkin's stomachs and shoulders, they cried out and shielded their faces. Many stumbled backward, caught off-guard. Some flew into a rage and lashed out, accidentally striking their own. When the second and third groups of archers united from the rear, the giants retreated inwards towards each other, their bodies filled with arrows. They were cut off.

Arlyn rallied his warriors to push against the shocked and increasingly wounded creatures. The chief managed to assemble a pincer move, in which they surrounded the yelkin, then worked at closing them, moving his warriors together towards the middle. In the face of so much brutal bloodshed, the Cathyrnee kept their heads this time, having regrouped enough to counterattack. Some of the yelkin fell to their knees, their chests glistening with blood. The sight of this sent the rest of them into a panic, and they fled, many carrying broken-off swords in their legs.

A tremendous cheer went up—a most glorious noise—as the archers mounted their horses and joined the other warriors to give chase. Arlyn's spirit soared from pride and relief before noticing the number of dead Cathyrnee dotting the terrain, littered among the smoking, smoldering remnants of their camp.

Arlyn searched the field for Gish, having lost sight of him in the bedlam. He found his top warrior lying face up and spread-eagled, his neck bent at a wrong angle, his chin resting further behind his shoulder than what should've been possible. A fly zigzagged across his forehead.

Tears clouded Arlyn's vision as he overlooked the field of pulverized huts. Even from this distance, he could make out his own hut, or what was left of it. Splintered poles made a pointy tarp of ripped animal hides.

Yarlaa.

SARNA

Her life was saved by the stuttering cadence of a chicken. After walking the entire night and morning through the Aimaar Forest with no food or water, Sarna became ravenous with hunger, desperate for drink. Her tunic was soaked in sweat and swamp water, her arms and ankles covered in cuts and scratches, and she kept stumbling forward. One more step. Another. Keep going. But there were no more. Her legs wouldn't move. She collapsed onto her knees. She would've fallen on her face if her hands hadn't stopped her. She stayed that way, like a dog, summoning the energy to move, but it just wasn't there.

At one point, she'd considered retreating the way she had come to find Luca again, cursing herself for ever leaving him in the first place. Problem was that she had no idea where she was anymore. As she kept walking, she kept expecting Luca to pop up at any moment, as seemed to be his habit.

The isolation of her grueling journey, combined with the tree shadows that stretched into long, stringy webs around her, created wild and fanciful shapes in her imagination. She even became convinced she was being followed by strange woodland fairies, and could hear their tiny footsteps along her trail, staying out of sight, though she spotted the occasional bush shaking.

Her vision dimming, sweat trickling off her chin,

chased by fairies, she heard the chicken. She lifted herself back onto her feet, stood still while trying to determine the animal's direction. She listened for it again, and there it was. Straight ahead. After a couple of steps, she heard the most wonderful sound to accompany the chicken—a cow! There was a farm!

The only impulse occupying her mind anymore was the desire for water. Her tongue had become so swollen she could hardly close her mouth. Urged on by the animal noises, she gathered strength she didn't have and ran. Before long, a root tripped her, and she flailed onto her stomach, a graceless flop. She lifted herself and crawled on her elbows until finding her feet again. She resumed running, though with a limp now. Her right knee hurt. It clicked. Didn't matter, though. Help was close.

Sarna held little doubt she would appear to anyone as a wild woman escaped from an asylum, but there was nothing she could do about it. She needed water!

She limped past a wooden chicken coop and had to stop. Her knee stiffened and became uncooperative. She raised her head and noticed a man outside a barn. The man held a pitchfork full of hay and stared at her, dumbfounded, frozen in mid-toss. She was about to speak to him when a short, heavy woman emerged from a cottage a few meters away. She blinked at Sarna, confused, then went into a stance with her feet apart and her right arm bent. She straightened her left arm, prepared to defend herself. The arm was bandaged.

Sarna held a hand up, gasping from an ache in her side. "No, no, no. I mean you no harm," she said.

"Who are you? What are you doing here?"

"I am Princess Sarna. Do you know me?"

Sarna thought she could see the woman gritting her teeth. Sarna's presence was far from welcome. She realized her claim to royalty was ludicrous in these circumstances. The woman looked afraid. Then it hit Sarna—the striped warrior makeup Luca had put on her before their ambush.

"Oh," she said. "Sorry." She wiped at the makeup with the back of her sleeves. She realized she was likely only smearing the makeup into a black face mask. She needed to wash it.

"What's your name?" Sarna asked her. "Is this your farm?"

"I am Ulaan. Know that I am a Ghe-sui. I can split you in half with a word."

"Ghe-sui? You're a shaman?"

The woman named Ulaan nodded but retained her hard look.

"Do you know the Magshaa? Can you take me to him?"

"You are not Princess Sarna."

"I am. I swear it. I was kidnapped."

"Why is your face black?"

"It's just...it's makeup. It's a long story. Please, I mean you no harm. If I could just have some water?"

"Who kidnapped you?"

"Some outlaws. I escaped."

The woman narrowed her eyes. "I want to believe you."

"I'll work on it. If I could just have some water to drink? I beg you."

The woman named Ulaan gave her a lingering, skeptical stare. She told her to wait right there. She went into her cottage and returned with a half-jug of water. She handed it to Sarna, who drank from it greedily, letting the spillover gush down the front of her tunic. When the jug was empty, she wiped her tongue around her lips to get whatever water she might've missed.

"Would you like more?" Ulaan asked her.

"Yes, please. Thank you. You're so kind."

"So you're Princess Sarna. *The* Princess Sarna?"

"And you're of the Ghe-sui? I thought shamans could read minds. You know it's me, don't you?"

"Only the Magshaa can do that. When he wants."

"Can you take me to him?"

Ulaan stared at her, still sizing her up, still probably unable to quite believe this filthy, quivering, skinny young thing in her farmyard was the actual flesh and blood Princess of Tartaria. She scowled, not hiding her renewed agitation.

A rooster crowed, and Sarna thought she heard sheep bleating. No longer shaded by the forest, the sun seemed impossibly bright and ruthless. Everything hurt.

"Please," Sarna said, squinting. "I need your help. I'll make sure you're rewarded."

Ulaan smiled, but her face looked sad. She started in the direction of her cottage. "Come inside and get cleaned up first," she said. "You can't go see the Magshaa looking like that."

20

CHIEF ARLYN

After packing down the last remaining dirt piles for his wife's grave, Arlyn set out to find a headstone. He searched the surrounding battle debris and located a partial pole from what used to be their hut. He twisted the non-splintered end into the ground. He set Yarlaa's red-and-gold battle helmet over it. The helmet was grimy and dented, but it was the only item he had left of hers. After he stood and backed away, the pole leaned from the weight of the helmet. Arlyn went back over and drove the pole further into the ground. He retreated again and observed what a pitiful marking it was for someone he'd loved so dearly. He wept but recovered once noticing how many of his people stood near him.

Since their current site had provided the Cathyrnee with the only victory they had ever managed over the yelkin, Arlyn decided to stay put for the time being. Also, there were a lot of dead people and animals to bury.

From his periphery, he noticed a warrior approach.

"Chief Arlyn," the man said.

Arlyn saw the two dark figures. He instinctively drew his sword and held it pointed at the warlock. Next to him stood a humanoid being with ink-black legs that blended into blue at his waist, then turned white across his torso, all the way to the crown of his bald head. He wore only a loincloth and held a spear made from rock. Together under the morning sun, their dark forms stood in stark contrast to their environment. A crowd was already gathering; everyone halted by the sight of two such bizarre entities.

When Arlyn was convinced neither intended to attack him, he lowered his sword. "How did you make it past my scouts?" he asked the warlock.

Seelskan fluttered his fingers above his head. "Magic," he said.

Arlyn nodded at the black, blue, and white being. "What is that?"

"He's Fhamtem, leader of the Chotgor."

"Does he speak Xhenkhel?"

"No, but I can interpret. Do you have a question for him?"

"Not even one." He looked back to his wife's grave. "Get out of here before I have you both taken prisoner."

The warlock cleared his throat. "King Khilji is

dead."

"You told me already."

"Do you believe me now?"

Arlyn looked at him, looked away. He shrugged. "Prince Shayan will make a much more sensible king."

"Where is he? He's not here to help you, is he? *We* are."

"Whether I've invited you or not, yes."

"I've returned because I was hoping your thinking had cleared, Chief Arlyn. I've come to offer you another chance."

"The answer, wizard, is no."

"King Montrose and Queen Saraal will be attending his funeral along with every nobleman and tribesman of Burnya and Tartaria. Baal plans to attack during the funeral. While every head in Jyn is bowed with grief. They will never see us coming."

"So what do you need us for?"

"I have but only an army of beasts and barbarians. We need skilled men."

"You need strategic thinking to go with all that ugly, brute force."

"You need us even more."

Some Cathyrnee went back to what they were doing, resigned to the idea that their lives would forever be a series of people and events they could no longer understand. Other people stood in open-mouthed dismay, awaiting the slightest indication that their leader was in peril. The sounds of hammering and sawing encompassed the entire area, the song of rebuilding which had become the Cathyrnee anthem.

"We defeated them," Chief Arlyn told the warlock. "The yelkin. They ran away."

"How many of the giants did you kill?" Seelskan asked.

Arlyn regarded his feet. He tried to count, but he hadn't actually seen any of the yelkin fall. Arlyn swallowed.

"You didn't kill any of them," Seelskan answered for him. "You ran them off, sure. But they'll heal. They'll be back when they get hungry enough. Maybe more next time."

"You sound like you're gloating."

"I brought Fhamtem here to demonstrate that he's real. That he and his people are willing to fight alongside you. Help you take back what's yours."

"What does he get out of it?"

"He and his kind will get some territory somewhat better than a boiling volcano."

"How much territory is 'some?'"

The warlock took a step forward. "How many people did you lose?"

Arlyn turned to look at him but found himself regarding the Chotgor instead. This creature might have been offering help, but he looked nightmarish. His expression was utterly impassive. His black eyes sparkled with a red tinge, as though somewhere deep inside were the secrets of the universe. Or the destruction of it. It was unnerving.

"We lost more than I care to count, wizard," Arlyn said. "Look, if your Baal is so great and powerful, why doesn't he wave his hands around and just annihilate everybody? Be done with it."

"Because he's a spirit with spiritual limitations. He'll become more powerful the longer he stays."

Chief Arlyn slapped his thighs. "I only want my people to be safe. I want them to stop being mistreated. Will he do that for us?"

"Have I been talking to myself?" Seelskan looked with his seething, crimson eyes at Yarlaa's grave. "Do it for your wife," he snapped.

"How did you know this was my wife's grave?"

Seelskan motioned at the makeshift tombstone. "That's her helmet, no?"

"You remembered."

"I did. Are you all right, Chief Arlyn?"

"You care?"

"I do. Look, the yelkin will be back. Again and again. Wouldn't it be so much easier to fight with them rather than against them? Aren't you sick of suffering?"

"I most definitely am," Arlyn conceded.

For the first time, he saw a slight grin move across Seelskan's face. The warlock placed a firm hand on the Chotgor's shoulder. The multi-hued being looked at the hand, then over at those Cathyrnee who remained staring at them. Those who hadn't gone back to work certainly did so after falling under those eyes. The three of them soon stood alone.

"You also lost your top warrior," said Seelskan to the Cathyrnee Chief.

"Gish, yes."

"Not to worry. This—" The warlock patted the Chotgor on the shoulder again. "—This is your new top warrior."

Arlyn regarded the tribal man-thing. He swallowed hard, then grimaced. "That strange spear he's holding. Can that pierce through Tartarian armor?"

The warlock's grin became even wider, showing off rows of jagged, rotten teeth. He said, nearly whispering, "This spear can pierce through *anything*."

THE MAGSHAA

His Holiness retired early to his chamber to sleep inside a mostly empty temple. The majority of his flock had chosen the leadership of someone younger, with a deeper sense of self-preservation, more progressive. The Magshaa could feel how it still shattered their hearts to leave him, but the moment was dire. The Sünsü was simply too new for them. The Magshaa had done his best to teach his shamans as much as he could, but time was running out. He was too old, too weak, his powers diminishing by the month. He could feel it.

Sleep would not come to him, so he rose from his bed, went to the main floor of the temple. He sat in what he estimated to be the center and meditated there. Without the accompanying energies of other shamans, a sense of calm did not come easily.

He decided to focus on his commitments to this life. He would devote himself right until the end. He would nurture compassion, forgiveness, tolerance, and self-discipline. He would stay committed to the promotion of spiritual harmony, respect for the value of each respective being, even Baal's. Until his last heartbeat, the Magshaa would hold his post as the spokesman of the Ghe-sui in their struggle for peace.

He fell asleep. He slept late into the next morning, which he hadn't done in countless years. He was normally up before dawn. He might have slumbered later if not for a gentle nudge given to his shoulder. He opened his eyes to see Ulaan leaning over him, her brows bunched with concern as if she believed him dead.

He struggled into sitting and squinted up at her.

"Your Holiness, I'm sorry to wake you," she said. It was Ulaan. "Where is everyone? The animals?"

He noticed a young girl standing next to Ulaan, inside the doorway. Though clean, she still appeared as though she'd been recently dragged behind a horse. Her fancy tunic was ripped, her face and legs covered in bruises and scrapes, some still bleeding. To his eyes, she was any other young woman, alone, afraid, and abused by a world that had no use for her except what it could beat out of her. To his heart, she was royalty, a jewel of femininity, the type of universe-altering potential that only a woman could carry. She was Princess Sarna.

"To what do I owe this visit, Your Highness?" he asked her.

Her face brightened. "You know me?"

"You've been through a lot, Princess Sarna. Come in."

"Where is everyone?" Ulaan asked as she found a seat on his bed beside him.

He reached out and embraced Ulaan. "Welcome back," he told her. "I'm overjoyed to see you. No matter the reason."

"Everyone left?"

The Magshaa nodded, and his smile vanished. "Yes, for the Kholm Mountains. There they can hide. The thick woods and rocky mountains should make pursuit difficult."

"They're cowards!"

"No, Ulaan. They are simply choosing peace over war."

"But you're the strongest among us."

"Not for long, I don't think. How did you and the princess find each other?"

He motioned once more for Sarna to step inside. She removed what was left of her sandals and entered, unable to hide her awe at the abundance of religious imagery on the walls. Sculptures and pictures filled every space.

"She stumbled onto my farm," Ulaan said. "Your Holiness, she believes she may be blessed with the Sünsü."

Princess Sarna explained herself to His Holiness by first mentioning her dreams and how they often came true. How she could once move objects with her mind but always kept it secret. She recounted the last few days, from getting kidnapped to exploding with light and murdering a battalion of knights, about the inescapable, horrific guilt of that. She told him about awakening to find herself floating among the trees. By the time she reached the part in which her best friend was missing, Sarna knelt before the Magshaa, her cheeks flecked with tears.

Ulaan helped her finish by describing how the two of them had ridden her fastest horse the entire night to get here.

He reached out and cupped the side of Sarna's face. "You already know about your father."

She nodded.

"It is never easy to lose a parent."

"You saw his death, too?"

"I didn't, to be honest. We received a Shuudan scroll."

"He was a terrible man," she said. She winced. "I shouldn't say that." She lowered her head, shut her eyes, obviously ashamed of what she had said and whom she had said it to.

A furry, blue aura emanated from the princess' skin. The Magshaa looked at Ulaan to see if she noticed it too, but she didn't appear to.

"Why have you come to me, Princess Sarna?" he asked her, already knowing the answer.

"Can you teach me, Your Holiness?"

"What is it you want me to teach you?"

"To become powerful. To help."

"You wish to have power?"

"Doesn't everyone?"

"But you *have* power. You're royalty."

"And how did that save me from getting kidnapped and almost killed? That will never happen to me again!" The blue light around her became brighter. The entire temple lit up in blue. "I also want to help my people," she said. "I have these abilities for a reason, right?"

"You have been chosen. This is true."

"Will you not teach me, Your Holiness?"

The old man frowned, dropped his hand. The blue glow around her faded. "I wish I could, your Highness. I'm afraid it's simply too late."

"I don't understand," she said. "Too late for what?"

"Chief Arlyn of the Cathyrnee, in his desperation to save his people and regain his authority, has summoned a spirit without having any idea what he was summoning. A vast and terrible army seeks to march on your kingdom. The Ghe-sui have fled north in an attempt to avert their destruction. I implore you to flee there as well. Both of you."

Sarna's mouth seemed to work around several words before she could find the ones she wanted. "We have to warn them!"

"We tried, Your Highness. Your brother turned us away."

"You met my brother?"

"On his way to pay your ransom, yes."

This sent the princess pacing, her fingers fussing with each other. "I have to do something. You have to teach me! How can you refuse? Your Holiness, please!"

"It would've been the most wonderful pleasure to have you as one of my shamans, Princess Sarna. Maybe you could've been the most powerful Ghe-sui ever. But there simply isn't time. The dark army plans to attack during your father's funeral tomorrow."

Sarna went to her knees. She cried.

The Magshaa was wise and respected, but he was also human. Tears came to his eyes as well. He was no one if not empathetic.

The princess crawled until pressing her cheek against the top of his foot. "Please," she pleaded. "Your Holiness. At least teach me what you can. We have to help them!"

He bent down and tried to urge her into standing. His old bones crackled, so Ulaan stepped over to help. Once Sarna regained her feet, the Magshaa cupped her face again. Her blue light returned, however dimly.

"Get some rest," he told her. "For a couple of hours. You haven't slept. Ulaan will find you a bed and fresh clothes, and you can come to me afterward. I will show you as much as I can if that's truly what your soul desires."

"Show me now. I don't need to rest."

"You must. You have to be focused."

"I can do it. As you said, there isn't time."

"Just two hours, Your Highness. We can spare that much. You must rest."

Sarna sniffled and wiped her eyes. "My brother is a fool sometimes." She noticed the Magshaa's tears and wiped them away from his cheeks. "You're the only prayer we have left."

"I am weak and old, Princess."

"You look strong enough to me, Your Holiness."

He chuckled at this. If only that were true. He would never be able to train her to harness the Sünsü in only a few hours. It took months just learning the proper way to breathe. Showing her how to use her powers without enough training, then setting her loose to fight, could cause far more damage than good. He would be leading the poor girl to a violent, painful death. Perhaps worse. Then again, as her brother had mentioned, they were in a potentially world-ending last stand; what did they have to lose? She could be dead anyway without trying.

"Would the gods lead the way for years and years and then simply shut the door?" he asked. "Miracles are happening now and will happen in the future. Get some rest. We shall do what we can later."

The Magshaa retired to his chambers to catch more rest himself. He had just lain down when there was a knock at his door. He called for the person to enter.

Ulaan opened the door and bowed. "I apologize for

disturbing your rest again, Your Holiness."

"I know what you did, Ulaan."

She remained in the doorway, uncertain. She kept her hands folded behind her back.

"Enter and shut the door," he told her.

Ulaan appeared too nervous to even meet his eyes. "The Queen offered me a lot of money. More than she's ever given. I would need three horses to bring it all to you."

"And what good is that money now? Ulaan, look at yourself. Look at what that curse did to you!"

He grabbed her wrist and pulled her forward, turning her non-bandaged arm out. An infinite network of black veins stood out across her cadaverously pale forearm.

"I thought I'd protected myself. I was…I'm so ashamed," she said.

"Did your curse work?"

"I don't know…yet." Ulaan fell to her knees, and he held her. "I'm so scared," she said.

"Go to the Kholm Mountains with the others. Save yourself."

"My place is here with you. I could never abandon you. Not after what you did for me, Magshaa."

"You are still too young to die this way."

She raised her head. "You believe the evil spirit will come here?"

"He's already been here. We came back from our travels to discover every animal slaughtered. This put enough fear into the other Ghe-sui that they fled.

Exactly as he wanted."

"Every animal?"

"It took hours to bury them all."

Her face withered, and she fought the urge to cry. "And what of the princess? Can you really train her? Would she stand a chance?"

"No, but it doesn't matter. Her path is not with us."

Ulaan straightened her back, perplexed. She wiped her eyes. "But, Your Holiness, I found her. She came to me. Where else would her path lie?"

He rested a hand on both her shoulders. A rectangle of moonlight fell across them, spotlighting them in the pitch darkness of the room. "She is already gone," he said.

21

SARNA

Earlier, Ulaan had escorted Sarna to a room with no chairs or bed, only cushions. Later, the caretaker Baeri brought Sarna an all-vegetarian dinner with tea. After finishing every last bite of food, she did her best to fall asleep. Despite bone-deep fatigue, sleep eluded her, partially from fear she'd find herself floating again, but mostly from the anxiety caused by what the Magshaa had told her. Her home and everyone she loved were about to be attacked.

Sarna waited for new clothes to be brought, but they never came. She got up from the floor and left the room through a sliding, paper-screen door. She went down the hallway to the communal bath where she gave herself a quick but thorough washing. This only worked to make her feel even more awake, so she decided to take a walk around the temple complex.

The crisp night air smelled refreshing. The twin moons hung side-by-side in the star-stuffed sky. She closed her eyes and concentrated on levitating, just to see if she could do it again, but nothing happened. She wondered what her Ghe-sui training might be like. How powerful could she become? How revitalizing to know she wasn't just some spoiled, clueless princess. She had abilities and a purpose. No one would stop her.

She heard a noise behind her. She went to spin around, but an arm seized her around her waist, and the other hand clamped over her mouth. She inhaled his scent and knew who it was without even seeing his face.

SHAYAN

Shayan rode his horse back into Tartaria. He held his arm in a makeshift sling created from strips of tunic. Although encouraged to leave the arrow in until his wound could be properly treated, Shayan decided it simply wouldn't do to saunter through the kingdom with an arrow jutting from his arm.

For protection, two knights rode on either side of the prince. Meanwhile, he noticed something unusual in the face of every civilian he passed. People bowed to him, but with an expression of profound despondency. He assumed their grievance to be caused by the sight of their wounded prince. He nodded at each of them, appreciative, but this soon changed into annoyance. He didn't feel comfortable with so much pity being leveled at him. He wasn't accustomed to it.

At the castle gates, Shayan handed the reins of his horse to an attendant. He took off his helmet. He commanded both knights to freshen and feed themselves, then recruit more of their comrades to help track down the princess. Inside the castle, Shayan felt slightly better. His arm still hurt, but he decided to lie down before seeking a healer. He had to deliver his bad news to his mother, the Queen. Get it over with.

Walking the halls, Shayan observed that the mood inside the castle was even worse than outside. An oppressive hush filled every stone. Those he passed bowed, but without looking at him. Shayan finally sensed something worse than the sight of his injured arm was afoot.

He asked an attendant as to the whereabouts of his mother and was directed to her chambers, where he'd been heading anyway. He found Queen Abika in the same spot he'd left her in—sitting by her window, only drinking straight from a bottle of babsulisk this time. No goblet.

Queen Abika turned at the sound of him entering. She greeted him with her eyes red and puffy. Those same eyes widened at the sight of his sling.

"What happened to you?" she asked her son, her voice croaking.

"I'll be fine. What's going on around here?"

"Where is your sister?"

"They didn't have her. We met with the bandits, but…"

Before he could finish, the Queen's face compressed to its center, and she broke into sobs. Her right fist, already holding a silk handkerchief, went to her forehead.

"I'm going to get her back," Shayan said. "I swear to you. You don't—"

"Your father is dead."

"He's…what?"

"He jumped out the window. Right in front of me. I couldn't stop him."

The prince couldn't move. The concept of his father no longer living seemed far too abstract for him to feel affected by. It was too absurd. "Out the window?" he asked. "When?"

The Queen told him what had happened. How she had awoken to the king in mid-argument with the fireplace. How she had left the bed to get help, but she wasn't fast enough.

Shayan didn't know what else to do, so he went to his mother. He embraced her while she sat, and she cried into his stomach, taking full-throated gulps.

"Your sister—" the Queen wheezed. "Where is Sarna? Who has her now?"

He took the bottle of babsulisk out of her other hand, set it down gently on the vanity table. "I will get Sarna back. I don't know what else to tell you."

"What went wrong?"

"They claimed she seduced their leader, and now they're on the run together. That's what they told me."

"Who told you?"

"The men who kidnapped her."

"That's ridiculous! Sarna can be selfish, but that's beyond even her."

"That's why we killed all of them. For lying."

Queen Abika went silent from this revelation. Shayan watched his mother as her mind tried to block the knowledge that her son had just killed people. That her daughter might be lost forever.

"Father was arguing with the fireplace? What was he saying?"

"Just nonsense. His madness got the better of him. We should've seen this coming. I should've done something more."

"It's not your fault."

The Queen moved her head back, looked up at his face. "You're going to be the new king, but you will still have to answer for killing Zov."

He paused, on the verge of denying the accusation. He decided to save time. "Zov thought we should get rid of Father by poisoning him. Had the audacity to even suggest it. Ohmaar will tell you."

"If you're truly going to be a king, you will rely on nobles to maintain power. Executing anyone, even commoners, will not put you in their good graces. Shayan, this is how rebellions happen."

"I'll stand trial. I don't care."

"How can a king stand trial? Who would try you?" She waved his words out of the air, disgusted. "The kingdom is too shaken right now for anything like that anyway. Pray it blows over. You're fortunate Zov has no immediate family."

Prince Shayan let the stark truth of everything his mother had just said to him sink in. To be king, he would need to be assertive and willful but always fair and level-headed. Never impulsive. Never again. The future of Tartaria was up to him now. Everything. Outbreaks of war, economic worries, mingling cultures, maintaining the hierarchy. There were likely other challenges he wasn't even considering.

He'd always felt he would be ready for this moment, but now that the moment was upon him, he wasn't as confident anymore.

He reached inside for the grief he knew he should feel for his dead father. He imagined him falling, the terror he must have felt as the ground rushed towards him. The prince felt nothing. Not yet. It was as if the king had already died long ago, a victim of his own mind. Shayan ran a gloved hand through his hair and gathered his wits. All of those battles during the Great War. All of those lives lost. All in the name of protecting their kingdom. Declaring their independence. All of that suffering and sacrifice for the citizens of Tartaria, only to have their beloved king jump through a window.

"I have two orders of knights searching for Sarna as

we speak," he said, wanting to change the subject again. "They will find her. I only came back because of my arm."

"Does it hurt?"

"Quite a bit. Where is Father's body?"

"At the monastery. He's been washed and shrouded. Notices have already been sent out across the Three Kingdoms. Ohmaar is handling the funeral." Queen Abika drank from her bottle. She shut her eyes, humming as the nectar hit her nervous system. "You were probably one of the last people to find out about your father," she told him. "I'm so sorry about that."

"We'll have the parade of parades for him. I will make sure he's honored like no other man of Jyn ever has been."

"We have to find Sarna. We have to tell her! She has to be there!"

Unable to withstand his mother's grief, he left the Queen's chambers. He shut the door behind him. He stood there a moment and recalled the way to the monastery. He held his head in the hand of his one good arm. *Wait, his father was dead?*

Two guards stood there, pretending not to notice him in his distraught state. This scared young man. Their new king.

22

KING MONTROSE

In the caravan on the way to the funeral, King Montrose and Queen Saraal sat in the same carriage together. They crossed a bridge over the Ikhar River, a wide, wild waterway filled with huge granite rocks, over which thrashing, rushing rapids flowed.

After riding throughout the night, thus far in silence, King Montrose turned to his wife. "Where have you been?"

"You know where I've been."

"The witch tell you anything interesting?"

"Don't call her that."

"What, she's your best friend now?"

The Queen shifted in her seat. She adjusted the hem of her dress, so it didn't touch the carriage floor. She let her gaze wander out her window at the lush forest around their path.

The king laughed. "She must be telling you some fascinating shit. That's for sure."

"I'm trying to help us! You. Me. Our kingdom. Everyone. If you cared about your kingdom half as much as your whores..." She looked away.

And so there it was. Just as he'd been warned. She knew everything already. Queen Saraal wasn't a complete fool. How naïve of him to think otherwise. Of course, she knew exactly what was going on.

"I care about the kingdom," he offered weakly.

"I even know about the baby."

He ignored this. "No one is more important to me than you are, my Queen," he said. Did he mean this? For a moment, he thought he truthfully did. He must have. Why else would he have done what he did to Ozyan? He reached over and touched the Queen's arm. "No matter what, I've never stopped...my love for you."

"What do you plan to do about your child?"

"I have no idea what you're talking about."

"Let me know when you do."

More silence, except for the sound of horse hooves and idle chatter between the knights, their powder-blue plumes bouncing behind their helmets. The forest became thicker, the ground covered in vines and wildflowers. The bugs seemed bothersome for the riders, which made King Montrose grateful for their royal carriage.

"I had her removed from the castle and taken back to her village," the king said to his hands. "You'll never have to worry about her again."

"That was cruel."

"What else would you have me do?"

When she didn't answer, he looked up and saw she was staring at him.

"So it worked," she muttered. "Miracle workers."

"What would you have me do?" he repeated. He reached over and took her hand. He squeezed it. He thought he felt, just maybe, the slightest squeeze in return.

The caravan halted. A servant approached their carriage, and King Montrose opened his door. The servant was the same Shuudan Rider who had delivered the message that King Khilji was dead.

"We're going to give the horses a rest," the kid said. The king already couldn't remember his name if he had ever been told. "Would you like anything to eat or drink, My Lord and Queen?

"Bring us some tea," he told the Shuudan kid.

The Rider bowed. He disappeared down the line of carriages, knights, and supply carts. He came back moments later, carrying a tray holding two porcelain cups, a spoon, a tiny milk canister, and a teapot. When the king opened the door for him again, the kid held the tray in one hand while the other poured the tea. He added milk to the cups. He used the spoon to stir, only he used a circular motion and touched the sides of the cups continuously, revealing he had never poured a cup of tea in his life. He handed them their cups before giving the king a bashful look, a silent confirmation of his real purpose. Without waiting to be excused, the kid left and retreated to the rear of the line.

Montrose watched as Queen Saraal lifted her cup to her mouth. The rim contacted the edge of her bottom lip. He reached out and swatted the cup from her hand. Most of the tea splattered across the floor, with some splashing across the Queen's dress. Fortunately, the flounce was plush enough to keep the hot tea from burning her skin.

She stiffened, aghast, too afraid to move should the mess on her lap touch her. "Have you gone mad?" She brushed gingerly at the tea droplets pooling between crevices of fabric.

"That servant meant to poison you!" King Montrose shouted.

"What? How would you know?"

"The way he served the tea. The way he stirred it. He had no idea what he was doing." He called out to the nearest knight on horseback. "Find that boy who just gave us tea and have him arrested!"

The knight raised his visor and gave his king a baffled look.

"Have him arrested and brought to me!" Montrose shouted louder. "Now!"

The knight lowered his visor. He rode his horse towards where the kid had gone. The knight beside him followed.

King Montrose tossed his own tea out his window.

Queen Saraal sat there, still dismayed, her back

pressed against her seat.

In a little while, the knights returned. They led the kid by a rope that they had tied around his wrists. He had a difficult time keeping up with their horses, but he didn't resist. He hung his head.

"Did you just try to poison us?" he asked the kid, the now-former Shuudan Rider.

He glanced up at the king, confused. He looked around at everyone, not knowing how to act or what to say.

"Speak!" King Montrose yelled.

"Y-Yes, but I thought you…"

King Montrose waved a dismissive hand, and the knights yanked the kid away, shoving him back towards the end of the line somewhere. A third knight, his visor raised, leaned into the king's carriage. This knight carried a shield with the blue Burnya crest, showing the two moons joined by a sword running through them. This meant he was a commander of some rank.

"Should we have him killed, My Lord?" he asked.

"Take him back to the kingdom. Throw him into the dungeons."

"We're already more than halfway to Tartaria, My Lord. It would be easier just to execute him. He attempted to kill you both."

"Keep him tied and make sure he doesn't escape. Keep an eye on him until we get to Tartaria. I will decide what to do with him there."

"Are you sure, My Lord? I don't mind killing him.

If he dared—"

"No." King Montrose shut his door to end the discussion.

The knight walked to the back of the caravan, presumably to see about their new and unexpected prisoner.

King Montrose settled back into his seat. He noticed how everyone's attention had become focused towards the rear and what was going on back there. An excited murmur moved through the caravan as news spread about the failed assassination attempt.

"I still don't understand how you knew there was poison in my tea," Queen Saraal said.

"I told you. He stirred the tea wrong."

"You could tell just from that?"

"Of course."

The caravan commenced moving again. Queen Saraal resumed looking out her window. "Ulaan is a miracle worker. Pure and simple," she said.

King Montrose thought to ask her what she meant but decided it best to drop the subject altogether. The royal couple settled into the comfortable rocking of the carriage, the benign babble of the forest. Before long, the shade of the trees gave way to the northern edge of the Orgoon Plains. They were almost there.

23

SARNA

Awareness. Rushing water.

There was light. It was morning.

Sarna felt the grass against her cheek, the dew moistening her tunic. Her throat hurt.

She'd decided to feign unconsciousness as a means to later surprise him and flee, but she ended up passing out for real. She wasn't sure how long she'd been asleep, but it couldn't have been more than a couple of hours.

Her vision blurry, she lifted her head, only to slump back down again. She lay there and listened to birds singing. She also heard footsteps in the grass. Busy footsteps. She opened her eyes and saw Luca moving around by a river.

Sarna sat up and rubbed her throat. She recalled his arm around her waist and felt furious with him. He had been following her this entire time, tracking her. Meanwhile, she had been on the verge of learning her powers from the Ghe-sui Master until this lovesick, brain-dead bandit had deprived her of her only chance to save everyone. Instead, here she was deep in the forest again, thanks to the primal, selfish needs of some entitled man. He wanted, and he took, and now the world was doomed.

She saw Luca fishing with a spear, which consisted of a long pole with a forked end. To make the fork, he had split the end of the pole into four parts, then wrapped it below to prevent further splitting. He had wedged some sticks to spread the forks and sharpened the splits. Luca was crafty. She gave him that.

Sarna heard an animal snort on the other side of her. She turned to see the horse he'd tied her to, the animal likely stolen from Ulaan's farm. Or *someone's* farm. The horse grazed on a patch of grass, unconcerned with either of them. She felt grateful Luca had at least cut her loose and kept her untied.

She searched the ground for a rock or anything to bash him over the head with. She found the ideal candidate only a few steps away: a hand-sized rock, large enough to hurt and sharp enough to do damage. She was a moment too late in grabbing it, though. Luca noticed her movement, and she stopped. They met eyes, and he grinned. He was in a good mood. Perhaps the happiest she had ever seen him. The nerve of this imbecile.

"Good morning, Sunshine," he told her.

She noticed the source of his good mood. A pair of fish lay on the bank beside him. Their green underbellies gleamed, their scales flaking and bloody, having been pierced with Luca's spear.

"As soon as I can," she told him, "I'm going to knock you out and run away from you."

"No, you won't."

"You're ruining *everything*. I was supposed to learn from the Magshaa."

"Forget him. I'll teach you everything you need to know. I already started."

"Like what? How to steal and kidnap?"

"Go ahead." He placed his attention back on the river, a wide, gushing channel lined with muddy banks, sporadically perforated with moss-covered trees and sawblade bushes. "Use your powers. Bake me into dust."

She made an image of that, wiped it away. She stared at his back. "So you've been following me this entire time?"

He peered over his shoulder at her. That smile was still there. He seemed to relish the effect this smile had on her. "Yes, I certainly have been. I never stopped. I would've gone to the end of the universe, Your Highness."

"Stop calling me that."

"All right then… *Sarna*."

"Where's your bow and arrows?"

"Left them at the camp."

"That was smart."

"You're funny," he said without laughing. He relifted his spear. He waded into the water up to his knees, the spear balanced in his right hand. He searched the water. "You're crazy about me, too, by the way."

She got to her feet. "That must be why I keep trying to escape from you."

"Have to hand it to you, though. I'm the lightest sleeper you'll ever meet. But the way you snuck away from me like that? *Joppa!* Impressive."

Without bothering to lift her tunic, she walked into the river until she stood next to him. She remembered putting on this tunic to get ready for school all those mornings ago. Little had she known she would be wearing this same tunic for days on end. She looked at the swirling, dark water swallowing her legs. "I regretted running away," she said. "I thought I was going to die."

"Crossed my mind as well."

"I had to leave, though. I woke up that night, and I was floating in the sky. I have no clue what's happening inside of me, but it's coming out anyway."

"Your father is dead."

"I know that. How do you?"

"Some ranch hands. Everyone in Jyn knows by now."

She touched his arm. It was there. "You have to take me home, Luca."

"Wait." He handed her the spear. She held her hands away, indicating she didn't want to touch it.

"No, take it," he said.

"I am not killing any fish."

"You want to use your powers to save the world, but you won't even hurt a fish?" He stood behind her and forced the spear into her hands, just as he'd done with the bow and arrow. "Take it!" Sarna gave in, and she held the spear. He guided her arm as he spoke, "Extend your arm halfway out. You'll need that room, so you can thrust forward as far as possible. Attack in one smooth movement. Aim for the fish's head."

"What river is this?" she asked.

"The Magoi River. Runs all the way out to the Ayal Sea."

"I always wanted to see this river. This is melted ice from the Kholm Mountains."

"Explains why it's freezing. There's a fish right there. You can do it."

She gave the spear a few bounces, testing its weight. "I always expected this river to be pretty. I guess this isn't the pretty part, huh?"

Sarna focused on the fish, its pale form blurred beneath the water. She chucked the spear and missed. The spear stuck out of the water, swaying, then leaning from the river's current.

Luca's right arm enveloped her waist as he kissed her neck. She about-faced to tell him to stop, but his lips were right there. They pressed against hers, and she felt a tickly warmth through her core. She went lax as his grip around her became stronger. Their faces met in a quick series of kisses, passion elevating until his mouth found her neck, exploring her skin. His hands wandered her back until she willed those hands lower, his hands obeying, sliding slowly over her backside, feeling its gentle curve as it became her upper leg.

As if in response to their heat, both fish came to life and flopped their bodies hard against the ground, locked in a spastic dance that frequently collided them with each other.

Sarna's hands went to the buttons on his shirt as a large shadow passed over them.

"Whoa, wait," Luca said, always sensitive to changes in light and dark. He pulled back from her and searched the sky. "What was that?"

"A cloud?"

"Far too fast for a cloud." He checked a different direction, still gazing at the sky. "Do you hear that?"

She listened but heard only the thrashing of the fish. "What was it?"

"I don't know, but it was huge." Luca reached out and lifted the spear from the water.

He started running up the river. This proved to be too much work, so he headed for shore.

"Where are you going?" Sarna followed him.

On dry land, Luca half-jogged, half-crawled up a jagged granite embankment, covered in algae. He reached an upward slope in the rocks. He peered east and was hypnotized by whatever he saw there.

Sarna clawed her way up to join him, huffing with

frustration over how events had once again flipped. Another shadow went over the sun, then another. She squinted up to see that the shadows were shaped like giant snakes with wings.

She reached Luca's place on the high rock. There, she saw the main body of a dark army still a few miles away, crossing the Narlaan Plains yet visible enough from their vantage point. The valley's slope gave them a view of what appeared to be a massive movement of creatures, pockmarked by the occasional platoon of men on horseback. Flanking this macabre army were what appeared to be giant, red-skinned beasts with enormous horns. However, the most ominous sight of all was the three black drakksuks soaring back and forth overhead, their reptilian eyes glowing purple, each shrieking with the pitch and volume of a thousand hawks, like the yawning of Hell. Their enormous, seven-fingered, bat-like wings nearly dwarfed their bodies. They looped back around to keep from flying too far ahead of the army.

She looked to Luca, who was busy gaping at the same sight with a hand over his mouth. His hand shook. "What is going on?" he whispered.

"This is why you have to take me home," she said, the word "home" drowned out by the drakksuks' shrieking.

Luca used his outstretched arm to nudge Sarna back, keep her out of sight. "To do what? Fight *that*?"

"They're on the path to attack my family's castle,

the entire kingdom of Tartaria. The nobles and royalty in all of Jyn are there."

"And you want to join them? I can't allow that."

"I have to try. And I'm not your prisoner anymore."

"What are you going to do? You can't even use your powers on *me*." He looked back at the marching army of darkness, taking it all in. He shook his head slowly. "This is bad," he said.

"Don't you still want your ransom?"

"Ransom? Think your family's going to care about *that* anymore?" He looked up at the flying drakksuks. "Look at those things! Those are *drakksuk*. Nothing can kill those!"

Sarna shut her eyes. She formed an image in her mind of Luca being shocked backward, unhurt, but far enough away that she could flee from him again. She concentrated hard. She went harder.

Nothing happened. She had no power over him. She had no power over anyone. She opened her eyes as he grabbed her elbow.

"You're staying with me," he told her. "I'm not losing you again."

She believed him this time.

THE MAGSHAA

He felt the ground quake from the eastern perimeter of the temple grounds. He left the temple with Ulaan following him, having felt the same vibration.

He hurried through the Ghe-sui village and walked far off-grounds. He reached a granite ridge. Though he had felt them behind him as he walked, it wasn't until now that he looked back. He regarded the entire group of remaining shamans, about twenty-strong. The event was upon them, collecting them together in awe. Though they couldn't see the dark army with their own eyes, they could see it in their minds, clear as crystal. It kept the shamans silent.

A roll of thunder tumbled across a cloudless sky. The air went from warm to chilly in an instant.

"The drakksuk," Ulaan said. "What are they?"

"They're from the ancient world, long before ours," said the Magshaa, then louder to inform everyone: "I don't know how Baal got them. He likely commanded them to help, which means he's already stronger than I feared."

"Will they attack the temple?" asked a different female voice on the other side of him. It was Corsika. He was not surprised to see she'd stayed behind. She'd kept an extremely low profile since confirming the news of Baal's arrival here into this world. And her involvement with it. He knew she thought he was upset with her, but he wasn't. He was afraid such anger might approach hatred, and there was enough hate in that marching army.

"No, they won't bother coming here," he told her. "We're no threat. Not anymore. They're in a hurry to make the king's funeral."

He looked at Corsika when he heard her crying. He

placed a hand on her shoulder to steady her.

"I'm sorry," she said. "I feel responsible. I *am* responsible."

"This would've happened anyway, Corsika. The Dark Shulam have been planning this since they struck out on their own." He thought a moment. He said to her, "Thank you for staying."

She rubbed her eyes. "We should try and help them, no?"

The Magshaa faced his shamans. All eyes were on him. He could see the same question in everyone's eyes.

"That is the issue," he said to them. "Do we stay with our path of peace and keep our powers safe from war? Or is this a conflict we can't disregard? There's no question this is beyond the mere squabbling of men over land, independence, and hurt feelings. This is evil."

He thought of putting the decision to a vote but realized they would much rather just have him tell them what to do. It was what they were doing here ultimately. The Magshaa took a headcount of his shamans and noticed Ulaan hovering closest to him. He could see the effect the curse was having on her still. Her eyes were ringed in gray. Her lips appeared dry and blue-ish. Corsika appeared wet-eyed and just as drained, veins showing on her forehead. He looked at the rest. Saw their lonely stories, their journeys of pain and fear, always suffering the persecution of being different. These were good people. They didn't deserve to die in such a horrific way. They deserved peace for once in their lives. The Magshaa decided he would give this to them. Peace. He could do that much. What else were old wise men good for?

24

SHAYAN

The prince admired his reflection in the mirror. He tried not to be vain, but at his age and marital status, it was hard, even at his father's funeral. Besides, he was getting fitted for new clothes, doing his best not to howl in agony whenever the tailor moved his arm. Each time, the tailor nearly flinched to the floor, mortified at causing his Highness pain.

"It's all right, relax," the prince told him, touching the tailor's bald head.

His funeral attire included a tan-and-black combination of tunic, cloak, trousers, and leggings. Deciding he looked too fancy and soft, he called for a wrap-over coat decorated with chainmail. He wasn't particularly satisfied with this either, but he couldn't take the pain of getting fitted anymore. Also, it was getting late.

With Shayan's influence, and despite the minimum time available, King Khilji's funeral was projected to be the largest public gathering since the victory parade at the end of the Great War. Apart from King Montrose, Queen Saraal, and every noble of Burnya, there would also be representatives from every far tribe of Jyn.

This included the Tsyan, who allowed their women to carry weapons and serve as soldiers. He'd been a small child the last time he'd seen tribal people, but he recalled being fascinated with their tattoos. The Tsyan wore a strange alphabet, inked in lines, which formed individual designs on their faces and bodies. Prince Shayan gave instructions that they were to be treated with as much respect as the Royal Montroses or any nobleman. Their accommodations were just as elegant, despite their own lack of concern for this. They wore little clothing and lived in huts around the base of the Zavgüi Mountains. They still fought with spears and wore bamboo plates as armor. These were some of the people the Great Awakening simply hadn't bothered with. Tribal people lived off the land and nothing else.

Prince Shayan had also invited Chief Arlyn and Chieftess Yarlaa, with whomever else they cared to bring. Unfortunately, a Shuudan messenger was unable to locate them. They had moved one too many times. Shayan decided his first act as king would be to patch that relationship. Though once his enemy, he respected Chief Arlyn. The man knew how to fight.

Shayan believed the Cathyrnee—even commoners, even enemies in defeat—were more valuable alive. Given the power and profit gained by staying out of their conflict, Shayan genuinely feared that Burnya was the real enemy these days.

It never once crossed his mind to invite the Ghe-sui. They would just beg everyone for money and be filthy.

The prince walked straight to the throne room. He joined a small viewing of the king's body. This was held only for family, dignitaries, royalty, donors, and staff. Afterward, the king's coffin was carried by a procession of soldiers. They headed towards Tank-him Hall for a public lying-in-state, a tradition in Tartaria since their first king, Prince Shayan's great-great-great-grandfather, all named "Khilji." (His father had broken the chain of names by calling his son "Shayan." He never said why, just that it was time.)

During the procession, Prince Shayan rode the same horse he'd been riding when he was shot, an odd thought which came to him during breakfast. He held the horse's reins with one hand, his other arm clutched in a sling beneath his overcoat. He kept a jug of babsulisk tied to the saddle. He openly swigged from the jug when his shoulder ache became too much.

King Khilji's coffin was carried on an ornate, golden carriage, the sides encased in glass. Queen Abika's carriage directly followed. Besides the Queen, sat a girl with Sarna's long hairstyle and same body type, told to keep her head down so people thought she was the real Sarna.

Shayan rode behind.

Citizens lined five-deep along the stone main way, everyone there to pay their respects. Assembled in front stood the entire castle military, plus the most elite knights available, predictably displeased at not being invited to attend the funeral rather than work it. Shayan cared, though. He explained to them how he wanted the best for his father, which meant high security. Most seemed to understand. The knights he had sent to continue searching for his sister had yet to be heard from.

Approaching Tankhim Hall, the prince could discern people making a ruckus behind him, which he first took to be weeping. There were plenty of people in tears, some openly sobbing. He even considered that the wailing came from the citizenry noticing their Sarna was a fake; therefore, rumors of her kidnapping were true. After a few more steps, the commotion became bothersome enough to make him look, despite the intense strain this caused his arm.

Two castle guards in tunics ran through the left side of the crowd, not struggling to do so but shoving people aside, even children. It caused an enormous stir, but the guards seemed in a panic to reach the prince. Shayan held his hand up to stop the procession. Those ahead of him didn't see this, so they kept going.

"Prince Shayan!" the guard with the shield yelled.

His shieldless partner lagged behind while his friend caught up to the prince. He pointed towards the southern gates. "An invasion, Your Highness!"

An immense shadow flew overhead. The entire kingdom went dark until the shadow was gone. People cried out, alarmed. A soul-piercing screech split the air, and the human wailing intensified. Soldiers and knights ran, some of them getting knocked down by the onslaught of people sprinting for safety.

The drakksuk arched its body to make another pass. Shayan was shocked to notice that it held several people clutched in its talons. A second beast flew over, but much lower. Its tail collided with a cone-topped tower beside the Hall. Large stones broke loose and created an avalanche of debris that pounded onto the procession. People were crushed to death, one of whom was the knight riding ten paces to Shayan's right. The knight's body lay on the street, his upper torso smashed over stones by larger stones, every structure cracked open, coating the gore in white dust. The concussion of so much plummeting masonry was enough to make some people fall. Others kept screaming.

A third drakksuk brought up the rear, its underbelly peppered with arrows, most of them broken off. The glow from its eyes cast purplish-pink beams through the rubble fog. One of its wings clipped a different tower and knocked loose another cascade of rocks and limestone mixed with lumber boards. People dodged for safety, unsure of what might try to kill them next. Some ended up running back the way they had come.

Shayan fought to keep his horse under control. The noise of spilling wreckage and yelling was terrifying. His horse wanted to flee. The animal reared up, but Shayan held on, fighting past the excruciating pain that any movement caused him.

He assessed what was happening. It was an invasion, yes, but where had these creatures come from? His mind flashed to what the Magshaa had warned him. This was the witchcraft of the Ghe-sui. The old man was attacking him!

A pair of knights crowded the prince and urged him towards the castle, where he could find safety. The three of them made their way as fast as they could, but were halted by so many people attempting the same. Soldiers and knights raced about, trying to comprehend what their best move should be. Nothing in their training had prepared them for flying monsters.

The drakksuk curved back for another pass but halted just above the rooftops. They backstroked their wings until vertically erecting the full length of their bodies. Their mouths opened into fang-filled grins and released a funnel of hot-white energy over the crowd. Those touched by the lightning melted into mounds of charred skeleton and skin. The stench from this was instantaneously everywhere, stuffing Shayan's nostrils to the extent he nearly bent over and threw up.

The sun became intermittently blocked out as the drakksuks dove back and forth, emitting white rays which fried or exploded anything they made contact with: people, carts, horses, all of it vanished into a dancing wall of burning white light, forked with lightning.

Both knights with the prince were now pushing him to the point of nearly dragging him off his horse. Shayan could no longer even see his father's casket carriage. It seemed impossible that it could have escaped being blown up. No sooner had he thought this than he saw the carriage, left abandoned by its horses, tilted to the front by a missing wheel. The last thing he saw before rounding the corner of an alley was King Khilji's carriage split in two by a razoring bolt dancing by. The entire carriage collapsed in a cloud of black smoke.

Random arrows shot up from wherever an archer could get one off. These men leaned from the windows of every building, planted there for security. Though some of the arrows found a mark in a drakksuk's underside, they seemed to cause the beast no pain. Not even annoyance. Many of the archers were incinerated in a swath of white fire before they could do much else. Their melted bodies fell into pieces over the ground and the people below.

The prince rode with the knights down the alley, though it was also filled with people. Awaiting them on the other side was another street, also filled with Tartarians crying and dying. Cones of white light pulverized building after building and, whether limestone, sandstone, or wood, the structure imploded on contact. The streets were engulfed in clouds of pulsating dust, making breathing difficult but providing the prince and everyone else with at least some cover.

The endless screams of the drakksuk were sickening, every shriek followed by a bass-level groan, heavy enough to shatter windows. The sound was unbearable enough with his helmet on. Shayan couldn't imagine the agony suffered by those without.

He forced himself to stop looking up through the dust, trying to find the drakksuk and stop judging where their galvanic breath might fall next. Focus instead on the quickest, most sheltered way to reach the castle, if there was even a castle left. A group of Tsyan warriors ran in front of him, not even recognizing him. Shayan opened his mouth to call to them, but a single ray of light pierced through them, cleaving them into clean pieces.

A large explosion shook the southern gates, and a fresh round of shouting arose from the masses. Prince Shayan hid behind a garbage pile.

One of the knights yelled into his ear, trying to pull him along. "There's an entire army of yelkin, Cathyrnee, and some…tribespeople! They're still a few leagues off, but there's going to be nothing left of us before they even get here!"

The other knight's head exploded in a spherical

cloud of puffy black smoke. The ashes blew past them, some clinging to Shayan's fancy tunic.

"What should we do?" a knight asked him, appearing from nowhere. "My prince! We need to organize a defense!'

Another helmetless knight in the street dropped his sword and stood with his arms folded over his head. He wept.

Prince Shayan watched him, unable to move or speak. Another knight started hollering at him, but the prince could no longer make out anyone's words, lost in the drakksuks' shrieking. Something glowed in the street ahead, but Shayan couldn't clear his eyes. The dust was suffocating. He fell to his knees, choking. He could feel the intense heat of a fire growing near his face. He realized the fire came from Tartaria, every square inch of it. His entire kingdom burned.

KING MONTROSE

Their royal, ornate carriage rolled down the main way with the help of two particularly muscular Jyn horses. Riding at each corner of the carriage were the same four Burnyan knights.

The king held his wife's hand again. He felt at peace, as though this was what was meant to be. The two of them together. Attending the funeral of a rival.

You will always be my Queen. The words were right

there on his lips. Before he could get them out, their area went dark as some large object temporarily blocked out the sun, followed by another and another. There came an ungodly squawking from the sky, and the physical world around them lit up with shafts of incinerating light. The funeral procession became blasted with large groups of people either turned to dust, eviscerated, or set aflame. King Montrose stared dumbfounded as a man ran by, his face a mask of terror and intense pain. The entire back of his body trailed a plume of black smoke, his flesh dripping like wax.

Feeling like a sitting target, Montrose pushed his Queen to get out on her side. His own side seemed to have taken more damage, rubble already piling into mounds. Occasionally, a human extremity or unidentifiable body part would hit the ground from somewhere high above. Everywhere lay knights cooking in their armor. Rather than trying to comprehend what was happening, the king opted to sustain their survival first. To run.

Once out of the carriage, he led Saraal by the arm away from the street. Both kept their heads down yet still suffered the sting of speeding pebbles ricocheting into them.

Flinching, Montrose peeked around to determine the best direction to run. The street was a river of people racing for cover, holding their arms over their heads, hoping to avoid getting killed by falling stones or white fire. The Queen got shoved by someone fleeing past, and the king lost her hand. She fell. He called out to her, reached to regain her grip. A white crescent of crackling light sparked off from a larger spray and severed Queen Saraal's left arm at the shoulder. He stood a moment, mesmerized by her missing arm, before crying so hard that he couldn't make words. Her seared flesh smoldered. She looked at him as if to ask, *What's this then?* She tottered over and crumpled to the ground. He made a move to go to her, but another sweep of white death from above obliterated the rest of her.

King Montrose went to his knees. He attempted uselessly to collect his wife's ashes as they blew away with the wind. He tried to stand but fell back down. Another try at getting up, and a kneecap met his forehead, sent him sprawling onto his back. He became stepped on.

He crawled until he found the wall of a building, then flattened himself there. He felt someone's arm encircle his neck. He cowered until realizing it was the Shuudan Rider, the same kid he had betrayed.

"Come with me, Your Highness," the Shuudan kid said. The king still didn't recall his name. "I will help you."

Though the kids' wrists were still tied, he took the king by his arm. He led him in a sprint back the way the funeral procession had started. They were stopped by a sudden rush of people racing back the other way.

King Montrose saw them: Red, saggy-skinned giants with maniacal, lopsided smirks on their faces, a set of horns extending from their foreheads. Running between their feet were a mass of odd-looking tribesmen with white upper bodies and black legs with a blue middle. It wasn't until they advanced that he saw it wasn't body paint. These tribesmen weren't human. The Shuudan seemed to realize the same. He turned to run in the other direction with everyone else. He pulled the king along, except the king couldn't run anymore. He was already exhausted. The kid urged him along anyway, but the king resisted.

"My Lord, you're going to die!" he yelled at Montrose. "We must keep going!"

"Why are you even helping me?"

"Because…you are still my king. We must run, My Lord!"

Montrose nodded. He let the kid take his hand and guide him into a trot. It took everything the king had left inside him to follow even half as much as the Shuudan kid pulled him to. Three turns around three blocks, and the king was out of breath again. No matter how hard the kid tugged, Montrose couldn't go anymore, too out of shape. He collapsed onto his stomach and blubbered. He smelled garbage, burning flesh, and burning wood mixed with sulfur. The sky wouldn't stop screeching. Seeing no other choice, the Shuudan Rider had a seat next to the king and waited for him to gather his strength. When a man fell dead within arm's reach of them, the kid reached over and dragged the remaining part of the corpse over them, so they were partially hidden.

King Montrose pressed his hands over his ears and buried his face into the kid's back, but there was no escaping the deafening clamor of so much mayhem and slaughter. He was dead. He was sure of it. Any moment now.

CHIEF ARLYN

He rode at a leisurely pace beside the warlock Seelskan. In the distance, evening fell perhaps for the last time over the kingdom of Tartaria. Its buildings burned bright, creating a wavering orange nimbus against the night sky. Both moons and every star made their appearance above as though it were any other night. Meanwhile, the drakksuk swooped over the rooftops, spraying sparkly white brilliance from their mouths, dousing every corner.

"Where's the other Dark Shulam involved in this?" Arlyn asked. "Don't you have wizard friends?"

"This glory belongs to me," Seelskan said. "The rest of my kind will *beg* me to be a part of this. Once this is done. But with the strength of Baal behind me, who needs them anymore?"

Arlyn gave the warlock a sideways peek. "Who are you, Seelskan?"

"I am one who is tired of living in the shadows. Tired of being forced to live on the fringe, ruled by rich people. I seek freedom. Nothing more."

Having covered Tartaria in flames to the extent it seemed redundant, the beasts flew back and landed a few hundred meters away. Lying on their stomachs, they panted while thin ribbons of smoke and mucous excreted from their nostrils. They rested as the motley army marched forward into the kingdom.

"Do you have any control over those things?" Arlyn asked the warlock, meaning the drakksuks.

"Yes," Seelskan said. "They just came and rested because I told them to. I could even make them talk."

"Don't make those things talk. I couldn't take it."

Seelskan gave him a look and grimaced. "Too bad. That's a conversation I'd pay to hear."

Arlyn nodded at the kingdom gates. "Are we still going in there? The whole kingdom looks fairly demolished. Might be dangerous for us."

"I told you I intended to exterminate every last man, woman, and child of this kingdom, and I meant it. I intend to see it."

"My only concern is finding Prince Shayan. Let's head to the castle first. If he's still alive, that's where he'll be."

"I would applaud the opportunity to see that. You and Prince Shayan squaring off. After you kill him, we shall display his dead body through the streets. Destroy all hope."

"I'd say you've done a solid job of that already. We didn't even need the volcano people and those giants, did we?"

"No, we absolutely do. The drakksuk will get annoyed if we make them do everything. They're selfish animals and quickly bored. Also, if they get too tired, they'll leave. I can only control them for so long."

Arlyn and the warlock reached the gates, already busted open and littered with smoking body parts. They rode in, followed by other Cathyrnee and the yelkin and Chotgor. Once inside, the giants and volcano tribesmen set about killing every living thing in sight. Those not out in the open were dragged from their homes and either speared to death, hacked to death, or pulled apart. Some of the yelkin used their height to pull families from the higher windows, often smashing the sides of their fists against the wall. This caused the building's facade to slide away from the rest of the structure, filling the streets with wreckage.

Block by block, the Cathyrnee walked along, stunned witnesses to the creatures slaying everyone. Arlyn saw how his warriors were made timid by the ruthless ferocity of these monsters who had somehow become allied with them. To Arlyn's slight dismay, his men appeared bothered by the bloodlust. They held their longswords but failed to begin their part in the butchering.

Through the dust, smoke, and fire, Arlyn did spot two of his warriors towing someone down the middle of the street. The chief would have recognized that huge stomach anywhere. King Montrose's body was limp as a rag, which caused Arlyn to believe the great King of Burnya was dead, but no—he was simply in shock. Or had given up completely. His tears made clean trails over his fat, heavily dusted cheeks. The warriors dropped the king at the feet of Arlyn's horse.

"My Lord!" Chief Arlyn said to him. "So sorry we have to see each other again like this."

The chief unsaddled from his horse and walked to where King Montrose lay face down. The King of Burnya kept his head lowered and used his elbows to crawl towards Arlyn. After reaching him, he embraced Arlyn's ankles. The king's shoulders shook as he wept.

Arlyn reached down and snatched the fat king by what was left of his hair. He forced him to his feet.

"Please, please, please," Montrose said. "I'll do whatever you want. Just tell me what to do, and I'll do it. Anything."

"I imagine you would." Arlyn gave the king a quick, hard shake. "Relax, My Lord! We're not here for you."

"Those monsters killed the Queen! My Saraal is dead!"

"That wasn't supposed to happen. I am truly sorry. Sort of."

"Are you going to kill me?"

"Why would we kill you? Burnya has always had our back, right?"

King Montrose seemed uncertain of how to answer,

uncertain of Arlyn's subtext. Burnya was widely criticized for never having anyone's back. The king settled on nodding. A string of drool dangled from his chin and moved with his head.

The chief became disgusted and slapped the king's face. "Go home, you worm. I'll have these warriors escort you." Arlyn laughed again. "Cheer up! It's a new world. We're not going to have to deal with scum like the Tartarians anymore. We *are* going to annex Burnya, though."

Montrose pulled his way to his feet. He wobbled but stayed standing. "You're stripping me of my crown?"

"That is correct, you hedonistic cow. Otherwise, we will have the drakksuk come give your kingdom a visit next. You can keep having your orgies, though, just not with the people you would prefer." Arlyn stood on tiptoes to address the warriors who had delivered the king. "Strip him naked."

With glee, the warriors ripped the king's garments from his body. Meanwhile, Arlyn went to a pile of dark ash and dipped three fingers in. Once Montrose was naked, Arlyn used the ash to write "LOVE ME" across the king's stomach, which elicited a hearty guffaw from everyone who witnessed it. "Now march him all the way back to Burnya," Arlyn told his warriors. "Make sure everyone in his kingdom sees him like that, even if it means your lives." Then to King Montrose: "Do you happen to know if Prince Shayan is still alive? Have you seen him?"

"No, I—what?"

Chief Arlyn drew his sword and brushed past the king, no longer interested in him. Around them, fragments of gore rained from every rooftop. The street before him appeared nearly unwalkable from the volume of dead bodies and debris in the way. The army's primary thrust even had to detour around an entire block that was on fire.

By the time Chief Arlyn and Seelskan reached the castle gates, there was already a swarm of yelkin there. Some climbed on top of each other to make hopping to the other side easier. Other giants pounded the wall, trying to bust through with sheer force.

A regrouped band of soldiers, knights, and tribesmen offered stiff resistance from atop the castle walls, but they were outnumbered. Eventually, Arlyn and the warlock rode through a downed section of the castle wall. They made their way through fallen Tartarian fighters. The yelkin worked themselves into such a frenzied state that many turned on each other. Soon, their clashing overflowed until it included the Chotgor, and a massive fray erupted between them. The Cathyrnee became the only ones still fighting to reach the castle, more comfortable now that their opponents were not civilians.

After the resistance force was suppressed, Arlyn and Seelskan managed to reach the castle gate. A Cathyrnee warrior greeted them there.

"We have the prince cornered alone in a room," he

told them.

"Take us to him," his chief commanded.

After tying his horse to a corpse, Arlyn followed the warrior up four flights of marble stairs. He ran behind him as they went into a hallway, already filled with other warriors. A group of them crouched near a wooden door, swords drawn. A single Chotgor was there holding a spear over his head, ready to do his part. Arlyn crept to the door and cracked it open. He leaned in.

"Prince Shayan, this is Chief Arlyn. I'm coming in, all right? I only want to talk." He waited for a response. When there wasn't any, he pushed the door open more, keeping his sword pointed, ready to slash anyone who challenged him. The door opened far easier than he expected, and he tumbled in before finding his feet. The room was quiet and dark. It appeared to be a storeroom. Inside sat Prince Shayan with his back against the far wall. He held his leg while it bled profusely from just below his knee. He looked pitiful.

"Go ahead and kill me if you want," the prince told him. "I can't swordfight you like this. You'd defeat me in seconds."

"What happened to you?"

"Something went through my leg. A rock, I think. Everything was exploding. I was also shot with an arrow yesterday."

"Sounds like a rough two days."

"Rough week. Chief Arlyn, what is going on? I'm

sorry I missed our meeting, but you didn't have to get this angry."

"I'm not the only one who's angry, Your Highness. This rage has been building up ever since the Great Awakening. Since you and your people decided you were suddenly better than us and could secede, then just claim whatever territory you wanted. Look at you now."

"My sister Sarna was kidnapped," the prince said. "That's why I couldn't meet with you. I kept it secret because I didn't want my sister to live trapped inside this castle for the rest of her life. And I'm sorry for what my father did to your people, all right? You know I am."

Arlyn relaxed his stance, lowered his sword. "I do regret things had to happen this way. I wanted a duel. I deserve one. So I'm going to spare your life, Prince Shayan, but Tartaria is finished. You're Prince of Shit now. Do you understand?"

Shayan scooted up against the wall. He kept slipping. "Where am I going to go?"

"Go live in the woods with all the other rejects. Nobody cares."

The door opened more, and Seelskan entered. When he faced the prince, Shayan gasped at seeing his smoldering warlock eyes, steaming up and over his brows.

Arlyn said to Seelskan, "Can you make him disappear from the room and reappear in the Kohlm Forest?"

"No."

"How are we going to get him out of here?"

"We don't. We kill him."

Arlyn held his arm out as if to block the warlock from attempting any such thing. "No, we do not. Murder everyone else if you want, but leave the prince alive. Shayan is a decent man. Just born to the wrong family."

"That's not—" Seelskan went still. He leaned in as if listening to a far-off voice.

"I say he lives," Arlyn said. "Or allow him the chance to join us."

"But his bloodline has brought him here. They've had their chance, and they ruined it for themselves. Allowing him to live would only allow him to continue being a symbol to his people."

Arlyn looked back at the prince, considering him. "I would slay him with a swordfight, perhaps, but not like this. Not with him already wounded. It's dishonorable." He walked over and helped the prince to his feet. "Heal yourself and come back. We'll have a fair fight, and I'll kill you that way. You won't find a better offer, Your Highness."

"This is foolishness," the warlock muttered. "I said I intended to kill everyone inside this kingdom, and I meant it. Allowing the King of Burnya to live is one thing, but this…I will kill the prince myself. Chief, step out of the way. I will…"

Seelskan cocked his head. He looked at the wall to his right, his brow puckering, as though he were trying to see through the stone to some important scene occurring just beyond it.

"Something's wrong," the warlock said. "He's here."

25

THE MAGSHAA

He and his Ghe-sui shamans halted at the sight of the great kingdom of Tartaria burning like an enormous cauldron. Periodic bursts of flames lit up the sky, each brighter than the last. The old man stepped forward until his toes curled over the lip of a narrow ledge. He searched the heavens, then the ground for the drakksuk, but he didn't see them anymore. He heard the terrible neighing of horses in distress, saw a herd running with their haunches aflame, just as they had in the Ghe-sui's dreams. The Magshaa heard the same child's voice warning him to leave or die. The sky was a canvas of honey and blood.

He looked back to the inferno of the Tartarian kingdom. He spotted a pair of almond-shaped eyes glowing violet. He made out another pair of eyes and a third, all six eyes staring back. The drakksuks appeared to have found him, too, sensing him.

"Oh, no," the Magshaa heard a male shaman say behind him. "They see us?"

The three drakksuk beat their wings and took flight. They propelled straight up until vanishing into a lower bank of clouds. The Magshaa already knew what the beasts intended to do. A few of the shamans seemed to know as well. They turned and fled back down the hill.

The drakksuks cried out as they dove from the clouds, as straight as arrows, headed directly for them. The Magshaa stood his ground as the three beasts appeared to pinpoint on him alone. The center drakksuk opened its mouth, prepared to either roast or eat the old man. They were only a few hundred meters from doing so when the Magshaa bowed his head, shut his eyes. He made four small, rapid circles with his hands, fingers clenched, raking together a pulsing pocket of air. He threw his right hand forward and yanked it back. This created a flat, undulating force field that split all three drakksuk apart instantaneously. Their bodies spiraled to the ground in several, large but distinctly different sections. Their innards glowed purplish-pink as they gushed with churning white light, left unexpelled from their mouths. Once hitting the ground, their headless torsos thrashed wildly, their nerve endings still receiving messages for urgent movement.

The Magshaa joined his hands and pressed his palms together as hard as he could. A second force-field expanded from the old man and incinerated hundreds of yelkin and Chotgor still outside the kingdom, their figures dissipating on impact. Some of the creatures ran the rest of the way beyond the kingdom walls. The Magshaa pumped his hands against each other, and a third force field-pulse spread out and sliced through another aggregation of creatures who shattered like crumbs of glass.

A cheer went up from the Ghe-sui shamans behind him. Those fleeing had stopped and started to re-group.

The old man felt the last remaining bit of his power ebbing. Gooey ectoplasm dripped from his finger-tips, and his shoulders smoked. He tried to warn the shamans to stay back, but a portal was already gash-ing the air just next to him. The warlock Seelskan stepped through the rip in time, an opening which bled and oozed as a wound. Eyes blazing, he held a flaming sword that he used to pierce the Magshaa's heart. The old man slid from the sword and fell to the ground.

Before the shamans could escape, Seelskan held his fists above his head and produced a zigzag line of co-ruscating energy, which cremated all but three of the remaining shamans. One lay face down, groaning and wriggling. The other two slithered on their stom-achs. Seelskan walked over and placed his foot be-tween the shoulder blades of the nearest one, a fe-male. He stomped his foot to prevent her from going further. The Ghe-sui collapsed and hid her face in the dirt.

"What is your name?" he asked the survivor.

"Ulaan," she sobbed.

Seelskan reached down and pulled the fat woman to her feet, and the woman complied. "Did you come here thinking you could actually defeat me?" he asked her.

The Ghe-sui's face was hidden by a fright-wig of black hair, matted with mud. Inside that nest of hair, a single, vibrating eyeball focused on him, scared for her life.

The warlock knew without having to question her: she would join them. She was no threat. There was plenty of darkness in her heart already. He saw it. Seelskan stepped around her and walked towards the other remaining Ghe-sui, still crawling as if there were anywhere left to crawl to.

26

CHIEF ARLYN

He entered the Queen's private chambers, where a section of the wall was missing. The opening offered a sweeping view of the kingdom's smoking ruins. He walked to the precipice of the gaping opening in the castle, admiring the maze of shattered buildings below, the streets crowded with rubble and burning corpses. When Seelskan entered the chambers behind him, the chief said without facing the warlock, "I let the prince go. I think we've done enough damage."

"Where is he?"

"He's gone."

"We agreed to kill *everyone*," said the warlock. "Exterminate these vermin from the world and start over. Why would you allow the prince to live? You confound me."

"There must be over a million dead down there. Maybe more. Let it go."

Seelskan reached the chief's side and joined him in surveying the razed landscape. "The Magshaa is dead. I also killed every shaman that was with him, except for a couple who have both agreed to join us."

"That's wonderful, I guess. What's next?"

"This kingdom is yours, Chief. You now own the land from the Zavgüi to the Oroo Mountains. From the Ayal Sea to The Ihhar River. Not bad, no?"

Arlyn frowned. 'I wish Yarlaa were alive to see this. I know I should feel triumphant, but I feel…just hollow."

He saw a group of Cathyrnee warriors in the castle courtyard. Some tended to their wounds while others cleaned the flesh and blood from their blades. They kept their backs on the yelkin lounging close by. The giants feasted on people they had torn from their homes, which was too much for the warriors to watch. The Chotgor, meanwhile, had gathered around the courtyard walls, also keeping to themselves. It had taken a spell from Seelskan to make the creatures desist from fighting each other. Arlyn thought some of the Chotgor were looking directly up at him, though he was sure this was only his imagination. He was wrong.

"So the volcano tribe will get their territory," Arlyn told the warlock. "And the yelkin? What do we do with these giants now?"

"What do you *want* to do with them?"

"I'd like to get rid of them. If it were genuinely up to me. Unless you can think of a use for them. I hate them."

The Chotgor were still looking up at them, reacting as if they'd received a signal. A few began walking towards the castle entrance, holding spears. He noticed the yelkin regrouping, a couple even wandering near to where the Cathyrnee warriors rested.

"Something's happening down there," Arlyn noted. "The yelkin are looking at my men like they're just noticing them. They're getting too close!"

"They are not easy to control. It's true."

"Do something! Stop them!"

The warriors realized the yelkin were becoming too interested in them. They picked up their weapons. A few of the giants went down on all fours, ready to run. The Cathyrnee gathered into a defensive U-shaped formation. The yelkin charged.

"No!" Arlyn yelled. He grabbed Seelskan by the shoulders. He seized the fabric of Seelskan's robe in his fists. "Make them stop!"

"You violated our agreement," Seelskan said. "Letting the prince live was a huge mistake. And King Montrose? I'm having difficulty forgiving you."

Prince Shayan apparently took these words as his cue and leaped from the closet. Howling from the pain, he hugged the warlock from behind, but his grip only lasted a moment. The surprise was enough to keep the warlock off-guard.

Chief Arlyn jabbed his sword into Seelskan's sternum. He shoved the blade upwards, so it skewered his body, not stopping until it reached his heart. Seelskan started to laugh in astonishment, but his soul slipped from his body, leaving it to slump upright while impaled. The warlock's corpse plummeted through the hole in the chamber wall. He fell hundreds of meters until thudding against the ground, uniting with the pile of slain giants already lying there.

The Chotgor had teamed with Arlyn's warriors to battle them, and the difference was substantial. He considered the reason for their help and could only imagine these creatures instinctively knew the best ally. The volcano beings were experts in combat. They used their spears as both weapons and pole vaults, coordinating with each other to land astride the giants' shoulders, then puncture their skulls from behind. The points of their spears poked through the yelkins' mouth palates and gagged them. Once a beast had fallen, the rest of the Chotgor and Cathyrnee joined in stabbing the giant until it ceased moving.

The chief saw Shayan on the floor, the prince unable to get up again, yet another leader lying at his feet. If only Yarlaa were here.

"Okay, I helped you," the prince said to him. "Let me go. You promised you would."

When Chief Arlyn looked back at the courtyard below, he saw that the warlock Seelskan was gone.

ULAAN

The further away from the burning kingdom she got, the harder it was to see where she was going. The night was pitch-dark, the moons and stars smothered in smoke.

After the warlock vanished, she ran. Ulaan didn't know what else to do. The other surviving shaman had fled without even waiting for her. She followed for as long as her legs could go, but she eventually lost him. Ulaan walked alone, back towards where she thought her farm must be. She had sworn allegiance to the evil being, though only for the sake of sparing her life. All she wanted anymore was to go home.

Atop the nearest hill, she made out the silhouette of a tall man. He watched her walk towards him and calmly waited for her. She stopped when she could make out his face, or as much as possible in the darkness. She could see he had a handsome oval face with a slightly rounded jaw. The face was serene but focused, showing strength in the simple way he held his features so still. He wore a black shirt with a gray collar and gloves. He wore black breeches and boots.

"Hello, Ulaan," he said. "I was expecting you. Were you expecting me?"

She squinted. "Who are you?" she asked him. "Do you need help?"

"My name is Baal," the man told her. "Don't you

know who I am?"

She knew this was preposterous. The man was traumatized from losing his home. From likely losing his entire family. "What do you want from me?" she asked him.

"Hold my hand? Take me home with you."

"I can't do that."

"Don't leave me alone out here by myself. Please?"

She resumed running. She ran as fast as she could until she couldn't anymore. She saw the silhouette of another tall man standing on a small hill ahead of her. Soon, she could see it was the same person.

"Hello, Ulaan," he said. "I was expecting you. Were you expecting me?"

She screamed and sprinted the other way.

"Ulaan, always running," he sang-said. "You enjoyed performing that curse. Admit it."

Her arms windmilled, but it failed to help her escape any faster.

"I know who you are," she heard the handsome man's voice say in her head. "I have always known you. Nobody cares about you more than I do."

SARNA

Luca rode his stolen horse all night and returned to the Ghe-sui Temple by daybreak. Sarna sat behind him, both arms wrapped around his waist. This return trip to the temple was a compromise between them. He still would not allow her to join the battle, which she realized by then was for the best. By reasonable measure of what she'd seen of that army, she knew she would've fought bravely but died swiftly. He agreed to ride back with her to the temple to see the Magshaa at least. As soon as they rode up onto the grounds, Sarna could see they were too late. The entire place was abandoned—empty, dark, and still. Or so she thought. When she and Luca rounded the front of the temple, they were surprised to find a small group of shamans sitting on the front steps, sharing a jug of water. They bowed to Luca and Sarna as they rode up.

Sarna slid down from the horse. She walked over to them. "Where is everybody?" she asked them, despite already having a pretty good idea. The shamans appeared exhausted and sunburnt in their light-blue tunics, each with a shaved head and hair tied into a top knot. They blinked up at her.

"We were sent to warn King Montrose and Queen Saraal about the invasion on Tartaria," said the oldest-looking shaman. "They had already left for the funeral, though, so we just came back."

Luca dismounted and led the horse over. "You don't have more water, do you?"

The Ghe-sui, last holding the jug, handed it to him. Luca took it and passed it to Sarna. "Drink," he told her.

She did. She gave the water back to him. A hush fell over everyone gathered on the steps of the Ghe-sui

Temple. A warm breeze blew around them. The two moons shone in the sky; a pair of enormous thumbnails etched into a magenta horizon. Sarna gazed north, the direction of home. She wondered what was happening there at this moment. How was her mother? How was Shayan? Maybe, just maybe, they had escaped in time. She imagined the castle, her place of childhood, the only home she knew—to think of it under attack from a horde of monsters and evil men was impossible.

Wherever Lalya had ended up, she was likely better off than home.

Luca handed the jug back to the Ghe-sui who had first given it to him. He had a seat beside him, groaning from the tiredness in his joints.

Sarna was having a seat beside him when one of the shamans leaped to his feet, pointing. Others joined him and muttered nervously. Sarna darted her eyes, searching for what had everyone so panicked. Luca got to his feet and stood close, sleepy, more confused than her.

Shielding her eyes, Sarna squinted north. She finally saw it—a robed figure in the distance walking towards them, rounding a hill.

SHAYAN

The prince spent the night in the forest with a band of nearly three hundred survivors. In the morning, he became the focus of an impromptu ceremony.

Every survivor greeted the prince warmly. Shayan hobbled on his injured leg to greet each of them. With one arm, he embraced those who seemed to require it.

"Have you seen my mother?" Shayan would sometimes ask a person. "The Queen? Have you seen her?"

"No, Your Highness. I'm sorry."

Shayan searched the faces of those around him, as he had already done countless times, hoping somehow one of them might be the Queen. Instead, he saw the faces of the most random collection of citizenry imaginable. There were calm children and hysterical adults. Farmers and nobles. The elderly and infants. Clothed and naked. Somehow, most of the survivors of this particular group were women.

While greeting everyone, Shayan did come across one familiar face. She was a young brunette girl he recognized as Lalya, one of his sister's little friends. He knew nothing about her, except that she now held a baby, wrapped in mucky, brown blankets.

"I didn't know you were a mother," he told her.

"I'm not. I don't know who this baby belongs to. I found her crying on the ground when I was running."

He frowned and tickled the baby's cheek. He was about to offer to hold the baby for her, despite his injuries, but a man shouted from over the prince's shoulder. He turned to see it was Ohmaar, not only still living but somehow relatively clean and un-scathed, though noticeably dazed.

"We must crown you our new king!" Ohmaar said. He sounded drunk, which Shayan supposed was possible. "I will do the coronation!"

"Nobody cares about that anymore," Shayan pro-tested, but when he checked around to see who heard, a few people had already walked forward to watch. Yes, they remembered—Shayan was still their new king.

Before long, the prince found himself encircled by a crowd of long-faced, grimy, shocked people. While they might have once been in awe of his Highness' presence, they merely looked on, numb but curious. Although mortified by the sight of so many atrocities, they did somehow seem to care about this, despite their prince standing before them in utter defeat and pain, covered head-to-toe in dust and dried blood, only alive because their enemy had pitied him.

"Very well," Shayan said to Ohmaar. "Tell me what to do."

"I don't have the coronation memorized," said Ohmaar. "I'll mash it together the best I can. I'll need a scepter, though."

He walked off towards a barrel of underbrush. Halfway there, he stopped to pick up a fallen tree branch, which he stripped of leaves and branches.

By now, every person in their survival group hud-dled around. The baby Lalya held began crying, so she stepped away so as not to disturb the ceremony.

Struggling through the soreness, Prince Shayan knelt on one knee, and it sank into mud. A drizzle fell, mostly deflected by the canopy of large leaves above them. A mist gathered.

"Is your Majesty willing to take the Oath?" Ohmaar asked the prince.

"Yes."

He corrected him in a low voice: "You have to say, 'I am willing.'"

"I am willing."

"Will you solemnly promise and swear to govern the Peoples of Tartaria and other Territories to any of them belonging or pertaining, according to their respective laws and customs?"

At the mention of his once-great kingdom, Prince Shayan's eyes welled up, and he swallowed back a sob. He couldn't help it. The enormity of what had just happened struck him. It nearly caved him, but he held it together. The coronation was the moment he'd waited for his entire life, but never like this. "I solemnly promise," he said.

"Will you, to your power, cause Law and Justice, in Mercy, to be executed in all your judgments?" Ohmaar asked.

"I will."

"Will you to the utmost of your power maintain…" At these words, Ohmaar's voice cracked, and he hid his anguished face with his hand. "I-I'm sorry. Sorry."

"It's all right," said the prince. "You're doing

great."

Ohmaar dropped his hand. His mouth moved, but no words came out until he managed to say, "I don't remember the rest." Wiping his nose, he scanned the area around them. "We need a crown."

"Make it invisible," Shayan said. "My crown is invisible."

Still holding the scepter branch, Ohmaar stepped forward and gripped his hands out with the fingers curled around an invisible crown. He placed it slowly over Shayan's head. "I pronounce you King Shayan of the Kingdom of Tartaria."

He tapped Shayan on both shoulders with the branch.

The crowd broke into scattered applause. The baby was still crying, then squalling. King Shayan got to his feet and regarded his people. He thought of making a speech, but the words weren't there. None of these people wanted words. They wanted their homes and loved ones back, and he, as their king, could do nothing to give it back to them. He opted to make eye contact with those still paying attention. He placed his hand over his heart and bowed to them. When he looked back up, Lalya stood there with the baby again. The baby had quieted.

"That was beautiful," she said. She sniffled, her eyes wet.

"That was humiliating. What a pathetic display. Our lives are destroyed."

"That's why these people needed to see that. To see

there's still something left of us."

"I can't do this, though. I can't ever bring us back to what we were. Not from today. I have no idea what to do."

"If I can survive what I had to survive this week, then anything in this universe is possible." She hugged the baby to her neck, which seemed an agreeable arrangement for both. The baby cooed. Lalya made a small laugh and looked at her sandals. "I've never even held a baby before."

He touched her shoulder. "I'm happy you're still alive," Shayan told her.

"You too, Your Highness." Lalya looked solemnly into his face, the face of her new king. "I'm glad you're still alive, too. Everyone is." She handed him the baby. The rain let up.

He held the baby, struggled to find a position that didn't cause agony, and noticed the infant's eyes, caked in soot but shining. "I wish my father were here," he told the child. "He would know how to handle this."

"Maybe," Lalya told the new king. "Looks like we'll just have to settle for you.

EPILOGUE

SARNA

The figure lowered its hood. It was Corsika. Without greetings, introductions, or anyone having to ask, she explained what had happened. How Tartaria had been decimated. How she had fled for her life upon seeing the drakksuk, so terrified that any sense of dignity abandoned her. After the shame overcame her, she was able to gather enough strength to rejoin the fight. Instead, she found the Magshaa slain. The rest of the Ghe-sui lay dead next to him. Tartaria burned like a tinderbox. The lamenting of those dying would haunt her dreams for the rest of her days.

While listening, the tears flooded Sarna's eyes, trailing down her cheeks. Her home, her family, everything gone. Destroyed. Dead. She was an orphan.

Sarna felt lightheaded. She needed to sit.

"Are you all right?" one of the Ghe-sui shamans asked her. No one was sitting anymore.

She caught herself with a hand against the temple wall. "What am I going to do? Where am I going to go?"

Three of the other shamans wept openly as well. The idea that the Magshaa had perished was doubtlessly unimaginable for them. Unrealistic. Though her own grief weighed on her, she still felt sorry for them. She felt sorry for Jyn. It was the end.

Luca reached to comfort her, but she moved away. She didn't want to be touched. She didn't know what she wanted. She wanted to wake up and find this was all a horrible dream. She wanted to have girl talk with Lalya about boys while brushing each other's hair. She wanted to learn how to play a musical instrument. She wanted to sketch a strange flower.

Luca kept his voice low. "Come on, your High—Sarna. Have a seat at least. You look like you're about to pass out."

"I am," she admitted.

"So sit. I'll find you some food. Somewhere. I'll take care of you."

She sat on the front step of the temple and folded her legs together under her ripped tunic. She embraced her knees and lay her head there. Sarna shut her eyes but was bolted alert by the racket of ringing bells. The noise came from above her. She looked up to see a collection of bells fixed to the arch of the temple entrance. The bells swayed, moving without anyone touching them, as if by magic.

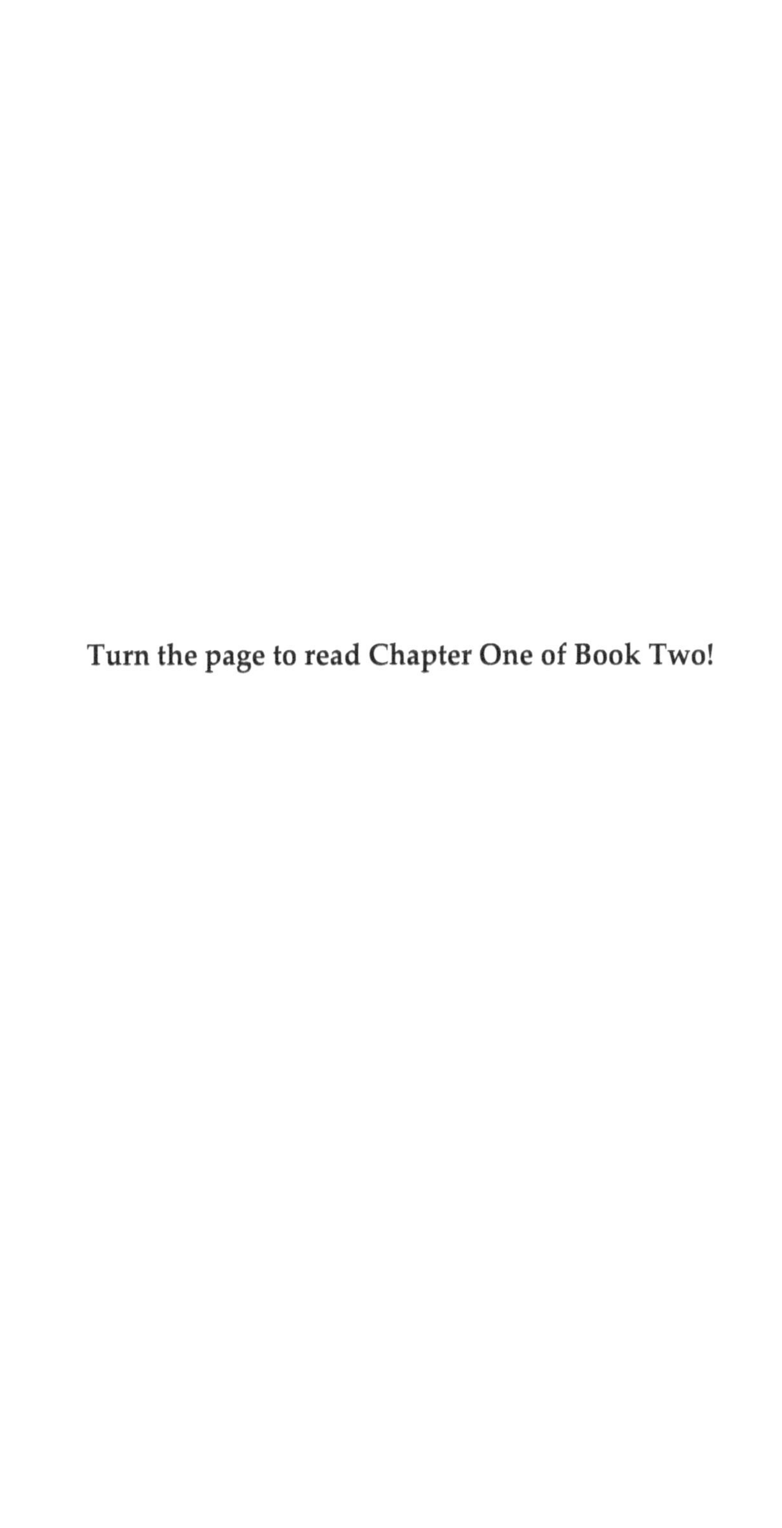

Turn the page to read Chapter One of Book Two!

BUT FIRST—PLEASE, LEAVE A REVIEW!

We would be extremely grateful if you could take a moment to write a review of this book on Amazon or Goodreads. Even a brief review (2 or 3 sentences) would be incredibly helpful.

Recommending this book to some of your friends would be great, too.

Thank you, and we love you!!!

CHAPTER ONE

THE APOCALYPSE WEDDING

LEE ANDERSON

1

SARNA

She held her arms firmly around Luca's waist. He steered the horse northward, an auburn haze at the horizon. High above, clusters of clouds hovered beneath a pair of thumbnail moons, the smaller moon peeking from behind the larger, its surface radiant and blistered.

Sarna's frayed, grimy tunic flapped against the horse's backside. Her exposed forearms and ankles prickled from the evening chill. They'd been riding for over an hour, and her inner thighs pulsed from the discomfort. She craved rest and yelled as much into Luca's ear. She was sure the horse needed rest as well. And to eat. Luca was pushing them too hard.

He ignored her. Sarna felt him leaning forward

more, kicking the horse to go faster. Though he had his moments, Luca was a stubborn fool. She considered the possibility that she hated him.

Their destination was the kingdom of Burnya. The bandit and the princess simply had nowhere else to go. Their kingdom had been leveled. The Ghe-sui had fled to the Kholm Mountains to save themselves. While hiding at the Magshaa Temple for four months, Sarna had no idea which of her family members were dead or alive. There wasn't even much hope that either of them would live much longer. Not in a flimsy, poorly-sanitized hut.

They headed to Burnya despite being unsure of where Burnya's allegiances lay anymore. Her father and King Montrose had always despised one another, so Sarna doubted the Burnyan king would show her much sympathy. Still, they had no choice. The realm of Jyn was overrun with unthinkable dangers, namely the drakksuk—flying creatures that breathed lightning. The Temple was also out of food. They needed civilization with fortitude and walls. They needed consistent meals and water.

Besides, the remaining shamans had chosen to embark for the Kholm Mountains weeks ago, joining the rest of their kind. They'd insisted the two of them keep the horse since Luca had stolen it.

Sarna pressed against him, their cheeks bouncing together. "We should stop!"

"Not yet!" he barked. "I want to make Burnya by tomorrow afternoon!"

"The horse is exhausted! I am, too!"

Luca remained focused on the path ahead. His long locks smacked her face.

After a while, he said, "There should be a river up here! We'll rest there, all right?"

"How far?"

"A few leagues! Twelve, I think!"

"No, no, no, that's too far! It's too far! Stop!"

He pulled on the horse's reins, far more forcefully than necessary. The animal grunted and dug its rear hooves into the ground. Sarna was nearly flung but managed to hold on by squeezing Luca's ribs. He cried out.

She went to scold him for nearly tossing her, but Luca held a finger up, signaling for silence. He swung his right leg forward and over. He slid down from the horse. He kept one hand on Sarna's knee, the other on the reins. He surveyed their surroundings, alerted by something unseen. A half-spherical hill bulged from the south, shingled with shards of granite. On their right stood a thin row of thick trees. The wind flattened the high grass in waves.

"What is it?" she whispered.

He shook his head.

She went rigid, listening for what worried him. She heard nothing but the wind until…voices. With Luca's help, she slid down from the horse to join him. The insides of her thighs throbbed, nearly sending her to her knees, her legs numb and noodly from the long ride. Thankfully, Luca caught her. He motioned for her to follow him as he led the horse into the shadow of the trees. Once there, Sarna stared with him in the direction of the voices.

The tribesmen appeared over a hill, less than a hundred yards away. She counted seven men in loincloths, doused head to toe in tribal paint. The luminous tint of the twin moons revealed the men in stark detail: Their legs and hips were black with a blue band around their waists and abdomens, turning to white over their chests and bald heads. They held spears. Their eyes smoldered with an orange phosphorescence, like hot charcoal, and Sarna realized these were not men at all. Her stomach dropped.

She and Luca held completely motionless as the strange beings walked closer. They spoke in a language punctuated with clicks and whistles, their cadence sounding far from melodic, but at a much higher timbre than she might've expected, considering the pure evil of their appearance.

Inevitably, their horse snorted and brushed its rear leg against a tree. The seven strange beings stopped and went quiet, their spears pointed.

Luca took a deep breath and stepped out from their hiding spot. He held his hands up in surrender. "Hello there," he said to them.

Sarna wanted to scream. Luca's recklessness was beyond comprehension. However, the befuddlement of these beings appeared to be what saved him. They appeared as astonished as she was.

"Didn't mean to scare you," Luca said. He dropped

his right arm but kept his left raised, as if swearing an oath. "I'm with someone very important." He nudged his head in her direction, then apparently lost his mind because he told them, "This girl here is the princess of Tartaria. I'm trying to get her to Burnya."

The nearest being growled, a low-pitched, demonic rumble.

"We wish only to pass on our way," Luca added, his voice faltering, likely regretting this plan already. "Do you understand? Are we all right?"

No one moved. Caught in a moment stretched from terror, Sarna noticed their spears were thin yet heavy-looking, made from what resembled volcanic rock. One of the beings pointed at Luca and said something in a jarring, idiosyncratic meter.

"Do you speak Xhenkhel?" Luca asked him. "I'm sorry, but I don't understand you."

The being with charcoal eyes straightened his back while sucking his bottom lip, an image so unsettling, Sarna felt sure she would remember it for the rest of her life, however short that might be. None of these man-things appeared happy to meet them. In fact, as a group, they appeared more than willing to slay them both for the first reason.

The same being who had spoken turned and spoke to the rest of his group. They resumed their advancement.

"What are you doing?" Luca asked. "Whoa! Wait! We mean you no harm!"

The beings increased their pace until they charged with their spears leading the way. They made no noise, no battle cry, only those glowing eyes narrowed with intent. The wish to kill.

Luca drew his sword, and the beings paused, momentarily off-guard, as though it hadn't actually occurred to them their foe might be armed.

The same being shouted at Luca.

"I have no idea what you're saying!" he responded. "Now back off! All of you! Let's please talk this out!"

Sarna held her breath and stepped out of the shadows. She stood next to Luca.

"We mean you no harm," she said, and saw no choice but to behold how dumb she was being herself now. They couldn't understand her! The only hope left was that they might interpret her tone favorably. Show mercy to a female.

They blinked at her, puzzled but interested. She took this as a good sign.

"Hey, friend!" Luca shouted. "Friends! Let's be friends!"

The being did the odd thing with his lip again, and he yelled. He raised his spear over his head, prompting the others to do the same. They continued their charge, their mouths open, revealing rows of slobbery fangs.

"Oh,…," Luca muttered. "Oh, no."

He became surrounded in seconds.

A veteran of Jyn's Great War, Luca had turned to banditry to survive. Both endeavors left him a fully skilled swordsman. Against his current aggressors, he used his longsword to slice along diagonal lines. He protected his sides while following through in a figure-eight motion, looping as he pivoted. Having such a long sword, he was able to cover himself and Sarna from multiple directions. Luca moved like a dancer, separating body parts in rhythm. The high grass became stained with gore.

Still, he was outnumbered. Sarna could see that maintaining such a whirlwind of movement required incredible energy. Luca feinted to one opponent while striking another. Unfortunately, while shielding against the first, or even a third, blow, he went to his knees repeatedly, and this began to slow him down. Even worse, despite losing limbs, many of the strange beings kept attacking, unbothered.

Luca blocked a thrust from a jutting spear but was knocked onto his back. He tried to get up and stumbled. He fell to his knees, inadvertently giving his blindside to them—the worst thing that could've happened. The three remaining beings closed in. The fight was over.

Sarna stepped forward. She'd only meant to make herself a flimsy barrier between combatants, but the world went white. A torrent of energy fountained upwards throughout her body, sparking through every nerve ending, webbing them with lightning, joined in concert. A cosmic sneeze erupted from her core, an all-consuming, uninhibited release of control. Her back arched and feet bent, Sarna exploded.

She floated just off the ground and gradually went higher. The ashes of singed grass curlicued in the wind around her.

She noticed Luca staring up at her, stunned and gaping. The strange beings were gone, even the ones already dead, reduced to smoldering stumps. Their spears lay about in scattered shards. A musty, sweet smell wafted in the wind—gases created from charged air. Sarna felt her hair standing straight out from her head, each strand repelling the other.

"I killed them," she said to Luca. She spoke slowly, entranced. "Every one of them. Did you see that?"

Luca remained on his back, trembling, his eyes locked on her floating figure. She recognized that look. She was becoming far too familiar with it from absolutely everyone.

He was terrified of her.

THE APOCALYPSE WEDDING

The Lost Books of Jyn,
Book Two

**Available now on Amazon, Barnes & Noble,
and other major retailers!**

OTHER BOOKS BY LEE ANDERSON:

WHAT HAPPENED AT SISTERS CREEK

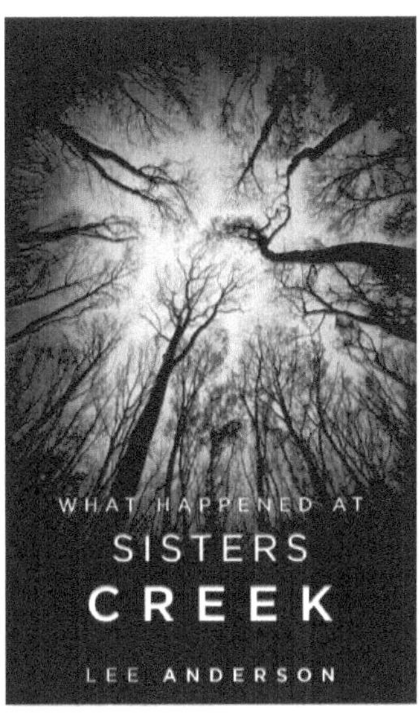

A small-town sheriff sends a search party into the woods to hunt two escape convicts. What they find is a savage, unthinkable horror...

"I squirmed, I cringed, I gritted my teeth and held my breath...And that ending.... I just.... WHAT? I don't even know what to say. Amazing? Exhilarating? Total WTF moment? It was soooooo good!" Jessica Scurlock, author of **Pretty Lies**

"It was VISCERAL for me as a reader in a way that all great horror/thrillers are. You want to be in it and at the same time you want to run the hell away from it as fast as you can!" Amanda Nicole Ryan, author of **Keeper**

Available now on Amazon, Barnes & Noble, and other major retailers!

This gripping collection of stories will take you on a thrill ride through a morally bankrupt landscape of desire, desperation, and constant danger. Dark Lords of the Trailer Park is an exploration of redemption in unexpected places. A riveting deep dive into the complexities of human nature, the triumphs, and challenges of society's outcasts. Lee Anderson's riveting tales will leave you breathless, yearning for more, long after the final page has turned.

Available now on Amazon, Barnes & Noble, and other major retailers!

Before You Go...

Thank you for reading!

Stories only survive because readers share them with others. If you enjoyed this book, the best way to support our work is to leave a review and tell a fellow reader about it.

For news on upcoming releases, exclusive previews, and special subscriber-only content, visit:

palmcirclepressbooks.com

We hope to see you again in another story.

ABOUT THE AUTHOR

Lee Anderson is an American novelist, short story writer, and playwright. He is the author of the horror novel *What Happened at Sisters Creek*, the short story collection *Dark Lords of the Trailer Park*, and the dark fantasy duology *The Lost Books of Jyn*, titled *The Atrocity Bells* and *The Apocalypse Wedding*. His two plays, *Supper's Ready* and *Little America*, were staged off-Broadway in New York City.

www.leeandersonbooks.com